'Why stare at me?' Stuart asked.

'You look so different.' Rosanna settled herself into the passenger seat. 'Such a change from those ghastly theatre greens. . .'

'With the trousers held up by string because the waist sizes would fit Tweedledum and Tweedledee laced together?'

Rosanna laughed with him, then stopped, surprised at herself for actually finding anything to laugh at while she was with Stuart.

Dear Reader

Welcome to Medical Romances! This month sees the innovation of an editor letter, which we hope you will find interesting and informative.

We welcome back Betty Beaty after a long absence from the list, and launch Margaret Holt with her first book, as well as offering Kathleen Farrell and Hazel Fisher—happy reading!

The Editor

Kathleen Farrell was born in South Africa, but the family settled in England while she was still a child. After working in a bank, she volunteered for the WAAFS and worked on the then highly secret British radar defence system. She married and brought up five children while working as a freelance journalist. Her daughter is a hospital surgeon who enjoys helping Kathleen with the medical background to her stories.

Recent titles by the same author:

NO TIME FOR ROMANCE

THE SINGAPORE AFFAIR

BY

KATHLEEN FARRELL

MILLS & BOON LIMITED
ETON HOUSE   18–24 PARADISE ROAD
RICHMOND   SURREY   TW9 1SR

First published in Great Britain 1992
by Mills & Boon Limited

© Kathleen Farrell 1992

Australian copyright 1992
Philippine copyright 1992
This edition 1992

ISBN 0 263 77658 1

Set in 10 on 11 pt Linotron Times
03-9205-52796

Typeset in Great Britain by Centracet, Cambridge
Made and printed in Great Britain

CHAPTER ONE

'I'M AFRAID you're in the wrong room. This is for senior doctors only; the junior doctors' rest-room is further along the corridor.'

Sternly, consultant Stuart Gainsborough—stretching to his full six foot two inches—confronted Rosanna Delroy, who had been about to sit down in one of the chintz-covered armchairs.

Undeterred, Rosanna retorted, 'No longer being a junior doctor, I'd say I'm in the right place,' while resolutely seating herself. Opening the book she had with her, nonchalantly she flipped through the pages and settled to read.

'You were a junior doctor last week.' Stuart stood squarely in front of her, his attitude bordering on the aggressive.

'Haven't you heard, Mr Gainsborough,' Rosanna resisted an impulse to raise a smug smile, 'I've been promoted to staff surgeon here, a permanent eight-hour-a-day job, no on-call nights. . .wonderful! Actually I've been given one of the few staff grade jobs in the country, no mean feat for a mere female!'

'Makes you feel unique, does it?'

'Triumphantly so.'

'And it's all come about because of you gaining a Fellowship of the Royal College of Surgeons?'

'That helped.' Nodding, complacently Rosanna turned another page of her book and appeared to study it in detail, although in point of fact she was not capable of reading a word, her mind concentrating instead on deciding what her next retort could be. Something crisp and telling, she decided—with perhaps a small dig at his pride since he had so little regard for hers.

'Because of their superior intellect women are encroaching on male preserves everywhere, Mr Gainsborough,' she remarked without bothering to look up at him. 'It's a fact of life which you must find very disturbing.'

Returning an indignant snort, Stuart retreated into the corridor, leaving Rosanna chuckling quietly to herself, gloating a little wickedly because she had so obviously succeeded in rattling him.

'He's so pompous!' she complained to Rhona Morris, a surgical SHO with whom she shared a flat in a hospital accommodation block.

'But impressive,' Rhona sighed romantically. 'I'm sure I'd have made a beeline for him if I hadn't already fallen in love and married Tang. Stuart's air of nobility gets me, and as for that aristocratic nose and the lopsided smile which comes and goes when one least expects it. . .why, it's no wonder the nurses get in a dither over him!'

Her brown eyes puzzling, 'Honestly, I don't know how you can bring yourself to speak down to him the way you do,' she continued more seriously. 'Aren't you scared of him lashing out verbally? I am. He can be very scathing when it suits him. . .but oh, with what finesse, such elegant skill. . .one can only stand and admire even while inwardly cringing. . .'

'You're crazy! You'd let him get away with murder! Or are you pulling my leg?'

'A little,' Rhona admitted, going through to the small kitchen to put the kettle on. She returned carrying two mugs. 'Tea or hot chocolate?' she asked. 'We're out of instant coffee.'

'Tea, please. I'll make it.' Rosanna half rose from her chair by the narrow gate-legged table.

'No, you sit there, I want to talk to you.' Rhona had

lost her buoyancy, becoming unusually grave. 'Have you heard that Stuart Gainsborough's wife ran away with another man, deserting two children too? That's why I'm always inclined to take his part against his many critics, I feel so dreadfully sorry for him.'

Rosanna shrugged. 'Don't waste your sympathies where they're not welcome,' she advised. 'I'm sure what you've heard is mere gossip from the hospital grapevine with no substance to it at all. You mustn't believe all you hear. But even if it were true it wouldn't excuse his chauvinistic attitude towards all women. Why, do you know, I think he was actually peeved to hear I'd been given the much desired staff job. Never congratulated me on gaining the Fellowship either. But don't let's talk about him any more—there must be other more pleasant subjects we could discuss?'

'But I have to talk about him,' Rhona insisted. 'It's crucial to my future. . .' She was interrupted by the shrilling of Rosanna's bleep.

Rosanna jumped to her feet, pushing her untasted tea aside. 'Tell me later,' she invited, before gathering up her white coat and racing back to the accident and emergency department.

'What's happening?' she asked the triage nurse breathlessly, in her haste almost falling head first over the nurse's desk.

'Male, aged twenty-seven,' she was told. 'Fell from a private plane. Landed on his left side against an iron bucket. No head injury.' The nurse put her ear to the emergency phone again. 'He's being brought in now.'

'Fell from a plane, yet he's alive? What was it doing, landing or taking off?' Without waiting for an answer, quickly, competently, Rosanna organised the injured man's reception into Casualty.

He was carried out of the ambulance looking pale, complaining of the pain in his left side, and having difficulty in breathing even though a nurse had provided him with an oxygen mask.

Rosanna had a listen to his chest through her stethoscope. 'Absent sounds on the left,' she informed her assistant Casualty SHO. 'Respirations about forty a minute.'

Checking the position of the trachea and the cardiac impulse, she found both were over towards the right. Having already called for emergency portable-machine X-rays, she asked the SHO to put up a drip, then, while nurses set up a chest drain with underwater seal—a drain going into a bottle with water in it so that air would not be sucked back into the chest—Rosanna prepared to insert the drain between the ribs on the left side.

When the young man's breathing had eased and he was noticeably less distressed, she asked him his name and how the accident had happened.

'Peter—Peter Armstrong,' he mumbled. 'I fell while I was getting into the cockpit of my plane. My foot slipped.' He winced then, his eyes full of pain. 'Oh boy, my stomach's sure giving me gyp!'

Examining him, Rosanna found he was very tender in the left upper quadrant.

'His abdomen's becoming rigid!' she told the new SHO in some concern, growing even more perturbed when the attendant nurse reported that his blood pressure was going down but his pulse going up. At that time too he stopped answering questions, becoming semi-conscious.

'Get the surgical consultant to come,' Rosanna called across to another of the casualty officers. 'It looks as if the patient has ruptured his spleen. Have eight units of blood crossmatched urgently!'

Increasing the flow of fluid through the intravenous line which had already been inserted, she introduced a second large intravenous cannula, getting nurses to use a pressure bag in order to put a unit of O-negative blood through the line without delay.

'Mr Gainsborough's in theatre. He and his registrar are completing an operation,' she was informed in answer to her urgent request for the consultant to come and see Peter Armstrong with a view to taking him to theatre for what she considered to be essential and urgent surgery.

'Get him to come to the phone. I'll talk to him, he's *needed* here!' Rosanna spoke unusually sharply in the stress of the moment.

'Surely your registrar can take over now and complete the operation in progress? This patient's life's in danger, it's a real emergency,' she barked down the internal phone into Stuart Gainsborough's ear.

However, even as she spoke the injured man's conscious level improved and he was able to start answering questions again, much to her relief.

'Emergency!' snapped Stuart Gainsborough, angrily sceptical when he hurried in a moment or two later and heard Peter Armstrong talking. 'What emergency?'

Rosanna ignored the outburst. 'The X-rays show fractured eighth, ninth, tenth and eleventh ribs on the right side,' she declared authoritatively.

Stuart joined her in studying the X-ray plates, then examined the patient's abdomen. 'Right!' he agreed briskly, becoming all surgeon again. 'Get him taken down to theatre. I'll do the operation myself immediately, but you'll have to spare someone to assist me. Registrar McCann will be at least another hour finishing off the operation we were doing together.'

Rosanna's face clouded. She knew she was the only member of the Accident and Emergency team to have had the necessary months of experience in what she was sure would turn out to be life-saving major surgery. She would have to assist Stuart herself.

But first, while a porter and a nurse pushed Peter

Armstrong down to theatre on a trolley, she took the opportunity to have a quick word with the senior Mr Armstrong, telling him about the injury his son had sustained and the nature of the operation about to be carried out on him.

Then she hurried down to the theatre complex to get changed and scrubbed and join Stuart, who was waiting for the emergency theatre to be got ready.

Theatre porters put Peter Armstrong on to the operating table, then, his skin prepared and towelled, he was anaesthetised and Stuart made a vertical mid-line incision, while Rosanna stood ready with a sucker to remove the intra-abdominal blood to help him see what he was doing.

Speedily he grabbed the spleen, detaching its ligaments until he was able to clamp the vessels leading to it and so stop Peter's dangerous haemhorrage.

'The spleen's hopelessly shattered.' Frowning, Stuart shook a concerned head over it. 'There's just no way it could be successfully repaired. It'll have to be completely removed if we're to save the patient's life.' Then, his voice softening, 'Say a prayer, Rosanna,' he suggested, much to her surprise, adding a grim, 'We'll need all the help we can get!'

Using their combined expertise, and with competent aid from the theatre sister and nurses, Stuart and Rosanna worked hard until finally satisfied that all that could be done had been done and the operation had every chance of being a success.

Exhausted, they more or less collapsed on to the bench outside the changing-rooms after Peter Armstrong had been wheeled away into the recovery area.

Neither spoke to the other at first, although as he rose Stuart rested a hand on Rosanna's shoulder for a brief moment, but whether that was a gesture of appreciation for her help with the operation, or a commendation, or simply a means of helping himself get back up on to his tired feet, she couldn't tell.

'Which is your changing-room now?' he asked, surprising her by his apparent acknowledgement of her promotion and altered status. 'Do you have one to yourself, or,' and looking up, she was sure she discerned a twinkle in his deep-set blue eyes, 'are you coming along to share the surgeons' room with me?'

'I share with the nurses,' she replied, rising also. 'In their cosy little élitest world male powers-that-be are still trying to swallow the bitter pill of having to acknowledge females as their equals, but they've yet to realise that equality doesn't do away with the physical differences. . .'

'Oh, surely,' Stuart interrupted with the semblance of a smile, 'being adult they must know. . .'

Rosanna found herself growing embarrassed. 'I simply mean they haven't got around to providing proper facilities for surgeons like me. . .oh, you know what I'm trying to say!'

'Well, don't get so stewed up about it. I don't like girls with bees in their bonnets!' Walking away, Stuart either chuckled or snorted, Rosanna was not sure which.

Changing back into her ordinary clothes but not bothering to put her white coat back on, she hurried along to Casualty, where she found quite a number of patients awaiting her.

'We've been rushed off our feet,' said Sister Helena Mills when the list had dwindled down. 'People coming in to show us cuts and bruises they've had for more than a week or so but haven't done anything about. One youth was so squeamish he couldn't look at his own scratches, others, mere kiddies, uncomplainingly put up with having needles stuck into them. Takes all sorts to make a world, doesn't it? Would you like a cup of tea? You've had a rough time of it with that young chap who fell down from his plane—is he OK now?'

'I hope so,' Rosanna returned wearily. 'His father was desperately worried.'

'I know. I saw him crying, so I gave him a hot cup of tea and a sympathetic nurse. Ah, here she is with *your* cuppa. I was sure you'd be wanting one, so I had it organised.'

'Thank you.' Rosanna accepted the tea gratefully and while drinking it, looked around. 'All nine cubicles of Area One are occupied, I see,' she remarked. 'Who's in that one with the curtains drawn?'

'One of our regulars, I'm afraid. he only comes in for a wash and brush up and a bed for the night.'

'Well, he won't get it tonight.' Rosanna finished her tea. 'We haven't a spare bed. There are too many folk taking advantage of us as it is—using us as B & B accommodation, then, when we have a real emergency to deal with, we lack the facilities.' She put her cup down on its saucer. 'Why's he occupying a cubicle?'

'Because his feet were smelling the place out. He'd quite deliberately taken his socks off to try to force some action from us. He's very cute—likes the girls to tend to him, but we beat him at his own game, gave our toughest male nurse the job of making him put his socks back on. He's succeeding, judging by the resentful expletives coming from behind the curtains!'

Buxom Sister Mills bustled away to greet an ambulance team. Rosanna went out to see what was happening. 'Painter fell off a ladder and went through the glass roof of a conservatory,' reported the triage nurse. 'Various cuts, some quite bad, also he seems to have dislocated his shoulder.'

Reducing the shoulder and picking out pieces of broken glass from various parts of his body took some time, then more X-rays had to be taken to make sure no glass remained embedded anywhere in the skin.

Finally Rosanna finished her task, only to be faced with a two-year-old who had obviously been abused, judging from the fingermark bruises around his ears and the burns on his hands.

Referring him to the paediatrician and social worker, Rosanna consoled the disturbed mother as best she could while insisting that the child be kept in overnight for observation. At that news the mother dissolved into tears.

'She's living with the child's father,' Rosanna confided to Rhona when telling her about the case while they were having a meal together in their flat a couple of days later.

'It must be quite a dilemma for unmarried mothers when their boyfriends take a dislike to the babies and vent their ill humour on them,' Rosanna reflected speculatively. 'Personally I think a mother has a duty to put the welfare of her young children first and foremost,' she continued, still in thoughtful mood. 'After all, they don't ask to be born. Everyone makes such a stand for choice these days, but *children* aren't given any choice even as to whether they're to be allowed to exist as far as birth, yet surely they're entitled to the same human rights as everyone else of whatever age, old, young or middling.'

Not looking Rhona's way, Rosanna failed to notice the distress building up behind those troubled brown eyes. 'Take that case I mentioned earlier,' she went on instead, growing really hot and strong on the issue. 'The mother maintains she's nowhere to go if her boyfriend turns her out, so she daren't protest too much, yet on the other hand, I'm sure she realises that if she and the child stay with him and he still can't learn to control his temper, he might well kill the boy one day.'

'She's caught in a sort of emotional trap, I'd say,'

murmured a strangely subdued Rhona. 'Perhaps she really loves her boyfriend and is afraid of losing him.'

'Well, she stands to lose both boyfriend *and* her son if there's the tragic ending we all fear. Anyway, now the social workers have been called in on the case, and because the mother is proving so hesitant about putting the child's welfare first, he'll probably be made a ward of court and transferred to a place of safety, so she might not be able to see him at all. The whole thing's very sad. Cases like this are happening far too often. They should never happen at all.'

'I know,' Rhona agreed, looking downcast. 'I too think the needs of young children should always be put first. If the mother can't provide a safe and suitable home, then she has no alternative but to let the child go to where he'll be well looked after. And that's my particular problem,' she added, half to herself.

'You're not talking about Song—your little boy?' Rosanna's quick ear had caught the unhappy muttering. 'Oh, Rhona, what's wrong?'

'Look at the time!' exclaimed Rhona, jumping up from her chair. 'I must get back to theatre! I've been forgetting I'm supposed to be on duty. . .you're lucky, you can go to bed!'

'What about Song? I've got to know!' cried Rosanna. 'Don't leave me to worry all night!'

'Can't wait.' Rhona ran to the hall door, pulling her white coat from a wall peg as she passed and rapidly feeling the large pockets to make sure they contained all the medical paraphernalia she needed to take with her.

'See you tomorrow evening,' she called back over her shoulder, and before Rosanna could reach the front door she was already halfway across the lawn outside the hospital.

After locking up, Rosanna followed, catching up with her by the changing-rooms. 'Quick, don't keep me in such suspense,' she begged. 'I won't sleep a wink! Is something wrong with baby Song?'

'Shush!' Rhona looked all around to make sure they weren't being overheard. 'I want time to think before I say anything more, Rosanna. Please understand and be patient. Look, I've *got* to get scrubbed up, don't keep me back!'

'All right,' Rosanna gave in with disgruntled grace. 'Just reassure me that Song's all right.'

The tenseness in Rhona's face gave way to a grateful smile. 'You do care for him, don't you! Thank you for that. He's fine, so don't worry about him.' She went into the changing-room, Rosanna following but keeping at a discreet distance.

'Think happy thoughts instead,' Rhona's voice came muffled as she slipped her theatre gown over her head. 'Like winning that free holiday, for instance.'

'What free holiday?' mystified, Rosanna called after Rhona as she made her way to the scrubbing-up sinks.

'The one the father of the chap who fell from his plane is giving as a thank-you offering. Can't wait—bye now. I'm off into theatre.'

'Giving to whom?' Rosanna enquired, raising her voice.

'To those whose names are picked out of a hat, I imagine.' Then, facetiously, Rhona called back, 'You never know, you might be lucky enough to be coupled with Mr Gainsborough!'

Listening, the waiting theatre nurses, amused, turned as one to witness Rosanna's reaction. Embarrassed, she fled before any of them could start asking awkward questions. The battle constantly waged between Stuart and herself was one of the main talking points among theatre staff, many a discussion being centred on the possible outcome, some intrepid young theatre porter even suggesting it might be worth betting on—one way or the other.

CHAPTER TWO

ASHAMED of herself for her inability to hide her feelings, Rosanna returned to the little flat to make herself a hot blackcurrant drink.

Think happy thoughts, Rhona had suggested. She often spoke with a wisdom beyond her years, so why not take her advice? Rosanna let her imagination run riot. A free holiday? To where? A coastal resort around Britain?'

She had been to most of them, not being able to afford to holiday abroad because, after her parents died so tragically in the rough waters around the Needles just off the Isle of Wight while taking part in a yacht race, she had found herself facing not only their loss, but also unusual funeral expenses, plus inheriting many debts to clear.

Three years on she was still having to watch every penny, being determined to repay everything her beloved but easygoing father had owed.

It was quite a relief when Kevin Berry called in to see her, distracting her from her anxious thoughts.

'What about this holiday prize everyone's talking about?' he queried, accepting her offer of a hot drink and afterwards carrying the two mugs into the small lounge where he squatted cross-legged on the floor in preference to moving aside all the papers scattered over the settee to make room for himself to sit there.

'Supposing we win it, the two of us, and the venue is some exotic place,' he grinned, daydreaming in happy anticipation. 'How would you fancy getting married under palm trees with hula-hula girls for bridesmaids. . .?'

'And monkeys throwing coconuts at us instead of confetti?' Rosanna laughed, then grew serious. 'I won't win it, I've never won anything in my life. I don't believe in luck. Everything I've gained has had to be earned the hard way, by determination, perseverance, sheer struggling, working extra hours, saving hard. . .'

'Ah, I hear violins,' sighed Kevin in mock sympathy.

'You're hopeless!' Rosanna dismissed him with a casual wave of her hand.

'Hopelessly in love,' he qualified. 'In love with a girl who hasn't a heart—now there's a tragic situation!' He ran a hand through his red hair, making it stand on end. 'If only I could be austere, impressive-looking like our surgical consultant, I might stand a chance.' He eyed Rosanna shrewdly. 'There's some truth in that premise, isn't there?'

'I don't know what you're talking about.' She stood up as if expecting him to leave. 'I like you Kevin, but if you're going to harp on the subject of that odious man, you'll be adding to my problems. I try to forget him as much as I can.'

'Sorry,' he said in an appealing yet hangdog way, getting to his feet, 'I didn't mean to upset you. I think the world of you, you know I do, but I can't help resenting the effect Stuart Gainsborough seems to have on you and I try, in my muddling way, to protect you from him. I guess that's it.'

Rosanna smiled, touched by his sincerity. 'Well, let's forget him and instead discuss this free holiday idea. Sit down in a chair and in a wise and dignified way air your views.'

'A tall order.' Kevin drew himself up to his full five foot ten inches, tucked a thumb behind the lapel of his white coat as if about to make a speech, but, unable to stay serious for long, abandoned the attempt, gave in and sat down.

'Let's make it a quiz,' he suggested. 'Where would

you want to go? What would you want to do? Go mountain climbing?'

Rosanna laid her emptied mug aside and shook her head. 'Haven't enough energy,' she claimed.

'What about a skiing holiday?'

'I don't think there'd be enough snow anywhere reachable at this time of the year, and anyway, I can't ski.' Stuart can ski, she thought, then was cross with herself for letting him intrude when she had no wish to think of him. Kevin was quite right, she decided, the formidable surgery consultant had far greater an effect on her feelings than she cared to admit.

Resolutely declining to let him preoccupy her thoughts, she asked Kevin to repeat the question he had just asked.

'I thought you weren't listening.' He smiled rather woefully. 'All I said was, what about a safari?'

'I'm not courageous enough, and anyway, I'm wearying of trying to tame wild humans, let alone animals!'

'That's a good one!' chuckled Kevin, standing up again. 'Especially if you're applying it to Stuart! I'll have to tell him. . .then watch him blow up! No, I don't really mean that, but I say, wouldn't it be great if more of the patients we treat could offer us free holidays, instead of threatening to sue us if we make a mistake!'

'Don't remind me of the schoolboy who came in this morning, a fish-hook embedded in the sole of his foot.' Rosanna pulled a face. 'I put in local anaesthetic and *very* carefully withdrew the hook, but all he did was glare at me balefully and shout "It still hurts! I'll tell my dad on you!"'

'There's no pleasing some people,' Kevin sighed. 'Well, I'll let you get your beauty sleep now. Do I deserve a goodnight kiss?'

'Not yet.' Rosanna turned away, adding perkily, 'You have to earn your place in the queue.' It was kinder to put it that way, she thought, than to air her more usual, 'I'm keeping that sort of thing for when I'm really serious with someone,' the excuse she had always before used to put off any aspiring suitors.

Kevin, however, was a good friend and immensely likeable. She always felt a need to be ultra-careful not to put a damper on his sensitive feelings.

She lay in bed that night thinking of the ungrateful schoolboy she had dealt with and how good it was to instead come across someone as appreciative as Mr Armstrong. His son Peter seemed quite nice too. She liked his friendly approach, his Greek hero type of looks, his sense of humour. It was no wonder, she thought drowsily, that the nurses spoilt him.

What a difference there was between Stuart Gainsborough and Peter! One so easy and the other so difficult. While Kevin. . .well, Kevin was Kevin. There was no one else quite like him.

She wafted away into a deep dreamless sleep.

Work continued at full strength for both Rosanna and Rhona for the next day or two, leaving them little time to discuss anything much, especially as Rhona spent every spare moment with her little boy, Song, who was being looked after by her sister-in-law down in the nearby village.

'Interest in the holiday award scheme has died from a lack of fuel; no one mentions it any more,' Kevin said one day, and Rosanna was pondering his remark as she sat alone one evening feeling rather despondent because all the nurses were full of their holiday plans, booking up here, booking up there, and all seeming to have someone to go with, while she had no one, and no plans to go anywhere.

It was her own fault, she chided herself. Kevin, the lively senior orthopaedic registrar, had made it very plain over and over again that he would make himself available to accompany her anywhere she wished to go.

She sighed, regretting the fact that, nice as he was, he couldn't 'light her fire', as the nurses so aptly put it. But then she had never met a man who could. Or had she? Quickly she closed her mind to thoughts of Stuart, deliberately settling on Peter instead, wondering if *he* would be content to be a friend without stirring up foolish romantic notions.

She broke out of her reverie when a knock came on her front door. As she opened it to find one of the theatre porters on the doorstep, her heart sank.

'There's been an emergency, an accident?' she asked. 'I'm wanted to help out?'

'Nothing like that, Miss Delroy. Mr Gainsborough sent me to fetch you to Surgery Ward Ten.'

What have I done wrong this time? was Rosanna's first thought, before she realised that the porter was asking why she was a Miss again after studying so many years to win the title of 'Doctor'.

'Purely because I've passed the exams making me a Fellow of the Royal College of Surgeons,' she told him as they walked along together. 'You know the way male surgeons are called 'Mr' and not 'Doctor'—well, females with the same qualifications become 'Miss', or, if they're married, 'Mrs' instead of 'Doctor'. I don't think they know what else to call us, to tell you the truth, and personally I'd rather remain 'Doctor', but I haven't any choice in the matter.' Her mind went back to Stuart's summons. 'Did he look very fearsome?' she ended by asking.

'Who, Mr Gainsborough? He never looks all that cheerful, does he?' was the porter's only reply.

Inwardly quailing a little at the prospect of Stuart taking her to task when she was already overtired, and rather dispirited, Rosanna heaved a great sigh.

The porter gave her a compassionate glance. 'Don't

let him get you down, Miss Delroy. You know, I remember the effect you had on us when you first came to this teaching hospital. You always had a smile for us. Lots of medical students start off by being friendly towards porters, but once they've qualified they don't seem to think us worth knowing. You've been an exception, and we appreciate that.'

'We're *all* equally essential, that's the way I look on it, no one more important than the other. The hospital couldn't run without people doing all grades of jobs, from cleaning out sluices to intricate brain surgery. I suppose even administrators are necessary!' Rosanna pulled a wry face, thinking of the one or two she knew who were giving the staff headaches.

'You mean we're like pieces in a jigsaw?' Joe thought about that for a moment. 'Little bits as important as big ones?'

'Yes, although I don't know that I'd thought it out as cleverly as that. But you're right—every piece is necessary if the picture's to be completed.' Rosanna turned to him just inside the hospital side entrance. 'Where am I to go, did you say?' she asked,

'To Surgery Ward Ten. Mr Gainsborough's there with that injured pilot.'

'Oh heck, I hope his condition hasn't worsened.' Her lighter mood checked, Rosanna put a spurt on and, nerving herself, hurried up to the ward.

To her alarm the curtains were drawn around Peter Armstrong's bed.

She halted for a moment, her knees trembling. What was she going to find? She put out a hand to the curtains, but for a moment lacked the courage to pull them back.

Suppose Peter Armstrong had died and it had been her fault? Something she had neglected to do for him, perhaps? How awful if she had failed him in some way. . .such a healthy, strong young man—until his recent injuries.

For the first time during her medical career she wanted to turn and run and not face up to whatever she was to find behind those curtains.

But, before she could nerve herself to put her hand out to them again, one was drawn back and there was Stuart looking down at her, his face more drawn than ever.

'We have news for you,' he said. 'Come along.' He widened the gap in the curtains.

Still she hesitated to look inside the cubicle until, to her immense relief, Peter Armstrong called to her from his pillows, and, to add drama to the situation, his father rose from the chair beside the bed to come forward, shake her hand warmly, and congratulate her!

'Why?' she wanted to know, completely bemused.

'Because the consensus of opinion is that you should be given the holiday of a lifetime.' Mr Armstrong beamed at her benignly. 'We all agree that the two surgeons who saved Peter's life should be the ones to benefit from the proposed reward,' he continued. 'You, young lady, resuscitated him immediately or he might not have lived, while Mr Gainsborough here performed the necessary operation with you assisting him. I have great pleasure, therefore, in providing you both with the all-expenses-paid holiday I promised.'

'To where?' Rosanna asked automatically after gawping with surprise, her grey eyes wide, their green flecks dancing with excited anticipation.

'Singapore or Hong Kong,' interjected Peter, smiling broadly at what seemed to be her happy reaction. 'I only wish I could come with you!'

'Why Singapore or Hong Kong?' Rosanna, still dazed by the news being sprung on her, turned to his father.

'I own hotels there,' Mr Armstrong explained with

some pride. 'You'll be fixed up in the best there is. All you have to do is to arrange time off. I presume that you and Mr Gainsborough have passports? Well, which is it to be, Singapore or Hong Kong?'

Rosanna stared back, all delight draining from her face as she realised she was meant to holiday with Stuart. Well, here's your let-out, her mind urged. Just claim not to have a passport, then no one will expect you to go. Say there wouldn't be time for you to apply for and receive one. You don't want to go on holiday with Stuart Gainsborough—you know you don't like him! Make excuses.

But she did have a passport, her parents had bought her one earlier on in the very year they died. The plans had been for them all to go yachting to Portugal, to visit Fatima. It would have been her first trip outside the United Kingdom, so, as she could not in truth deny having a passport, she nodded a 'yes' to Mr Armstrong.

'Well, I'm told you both have holiday leave due and Mr Gainsborough says he wishes to leave the choice of destination to you. . .so which is it to be?'

Rosanna was sorely tempted. Rhona's marriage to a Singaporean doctor had given her a great interest in the island, with a longing to visit it and see what life there would have in store for her friend.

'I'm sending the two of you together.' Mr Armstrong looked discerningly at Rosanna as if sensing a certain reluctance on her part. 'It wouldn't be wise for you to visit either place on your own,' he explained. 'Now tell me, is Singapore your choice?'

Rosanna glanced at Stuart, but his expression was impassive, so she said, 'Yes, please,' left with no alternative but to make the decision for both of them.

'Then that's settled, and I'll tell my secretary to set things in motion.' Mr Armstrong rose. 'I'm off to the States tomorrow on business, then coming back to collect Peter.'

Rosanna peered at Stuart. There was no pleasure in his face, so she guessed he was as annoyed as she was not to have been given any choice of companion.

Rather woodenly he shook hands with Mr Armstrong, thanked him for his generosity, waited while Rosanna added her thanks, then walked off with her, but as soon as they turned into the corridor they parted to go their separate ways, each looking as stunned as the other and neither saying a word.

Rhona failed to return to the flat that night, so Rosanna had no option but to keep her news to herself. The next morning, the Casualty consultant still being away, she took first the ward round, then the clinic.

It was a busy day, with no time for breaks of any sort. She lost count of the number of patients she saw before mid-afternoon when, famished, she slipped away to the canteen for a sandwich.

Much to her surprise, Stuart Gainsborough made room for her to sit beside him at his table. 'This is my first meal of the day,' he groused. 'The sandwiches are nothing if not stale. Look at yours! Both the bread and its slice of unappetising meat curling up at the edges, a sorry piece of lettuce trying its darnedest to escape but unable to summon up enough energy!'

'I think I'd better take it up to Casualty with me,' murmured Rosanna, trying to make light of his complaint and standing up again.

'Why be in such a hurry?' Stuart frowned, his brows drawn.

'There's a very distraught young mother up there,' she told him by way of excuse. 'She was coming downstairs carrying her eight-month baby when she fell, and the child shot out of her arms.'

'Will surgery be needed?'

'No, the baby just bounced, he's fine. The mother suffered a sprained ankle and a few bruises, but nothing serious. It's the after-effect, the realisation of what *might* have happened, that she can't get over. She's sobbing her heart out, so is the sister who came in with her. I'd better go back and see if I can pacify them.'

'Hardly a busy doctor's job,' Stuart commented scathingly. 'Can't the nurses cope? Or is calming histrionics part of a staff surgeon's duties?'

'I've other things to do as well!' Rosanna drew away, wondering why he always managed to get under her skin and put her so much on the defensive.

'Run along, then.' He waved a hand dismissively. . .just as if she needed his permission, she thought indignantly. 'But we'll have to talk about this holiday business some time,' he added without looking up again. 'Tonight at eight. You'll be free, won't you? Don't bother to bring sandwiches.'

Was he being purposely droll? wondered Rosanna. A twisted sense of humour, perhaps? And, not too sure how she was expected to react, she merely threw back a casual, 'All right, tonight at eight. Pick me up outside the accommodation block.'

She walked away feeling gleefully triumphant, sure he would have no idea *which* accommodation block. She had made no attempt to make his task any the easier by identifying her particular one, instead half hoping he would get lost among the many blocks, so sparing her the embarrassment of spending the evening with him.

'I never know what to say to him,' she remarked to Rhona, when they met to have a coffee together and catch up with their individual items of news. 'I haven't made up my mind whether to accept the holiday or not. I don't like the thought of having Stuart as a companion, but I must admit he rather intrigues me. I'd love to find out what makes him tick!'

'So you *have* been offered it. I thought you would be, or was your name simply drawn out of the hat?' queried Rhona.

Rosanna shook her head. 'No, the hat was dispensed with, the powers that be insisting that the two doctors who worked on Peter after the accident saved his life, so they should be the ones to have the free holiday. Nice of them. . . I suppose.'

In spite of her words, Rosanna's voice remained flat.

'Oh, I see,' said Rhona discerningly. 'So that means Stuart Gainsborough definitely gets the other ticket. Will you be going on holiday with him?'

'Will I heck!' Rosanna almost exploded with the words, adding a convincing, 'I'd die sooner!'

By this time the girls had reached their accommodation, and Rosanna went straight into the tiny kitchen to fill the kettle and put it on to boil.

'So you turned down the offer?' asked Rhona, following her and taking two mugs from the cupboard above the sink.

'No, I didn't—I lacked the nerve. It would have seemed too discourteous to have done so there and then. The Armstrongs, father and son, would have been very hurt. I'll have to find a really good excuse for not taking up their offer, an excuse they'll find easy to accept.'

'Did they tell you the holiday destination?'

Rosanna was making the coffee. 'Oh, yes— Singapore,' she said casually, unaware of the effect her words would have.

Rhona gasped, her cheeks losing their colour and a pensive look coming into her brown eyes.

For a moment she seemed unable to speak, then, slipping off her white coat and collecting an anorak she said, 'I'm just going along to see Song safely tucked up for the night,' and pushed her cup aside with an impatient movement spilling some coffee into the saucer in her obvious hurry to get away. Rosanna looked up at her as she passed. Rhona's eyes were misting over.

Never one to remain silent on any issue which caused her concern, she spoke out directly Rhona returned, coming out of her bedroom to tackle her.

'Why were you so upset before you went to see your baby?' she asked. 'Is he really all right?'

Rhona nodded but remained looking miserable, walking away from her into the kitchen. Not bothering to remove the anorak, she slumped down on to one of the two wooden chairs and humped herself over the small drop-leaf table.

'I have to find another home for Song, and I don't like him having all these moves—it isn't doing him any good. I wish I could get him settled once and for all. Tang's sister has been doing a great job looking after him, but her father's had a stroke and she must go back home immediately. There's no time to get a passport for Song, who has to have one for himself, so she can't take him with her. What am I going to do, Rosanna?' She raised a woebegone face. 'Tang can't get away from his hospital again, he's only just returned there after his holiday over here.'

'Oh, dear, what a pity this had to happen just when you're coming to the end of your six-month stint in surgery!'

'I know.' Rhona's eyes were filling with tears again. 'Actually I'd had a cable from Tang earlier on today, that's why I went down to the village just now, to see what his sister proposed to do.' She shrugged. 'You know the rest.' Her head bowed down miserably again. 'And I don't see how I'll be able to keep Song's existence secret from the hospital staff if I have to have him here. . .which puts paid to my chances of getting a good reference from my surgery boss, and if I don't get that reference I won't be able to take up the post offered by Tang's hospital. . . . I'm sorry I'm so weepy,' she went on, 'but it's all such a horrible mess!' She sought through her pockets for another tissue.

'Here, have the box.' Rosanna pushed it towards her. 'So now I know why you looked so miserable before you went out earlier on. Mind you,' she made a determined cheering-up effort, 'there's a light at the end of every tunnel, we've only to look up for it. What about that nice landlady where your sister-in-law's been staying with Song? She's been the soul of discretion, hasn't she, never letting on that Song was your baby. Wouldn't she help out just until you have that crucial reference and finish here ready to go and join your husband?'

'She's willing enough, but the trouble is she has an evening job, and a holiday booked for three weeks' time. . .'

'We could take care of Song between us in the evenings.'

'But in three weeks' time, what then?'

'I don't know,' Rosanna said frankly. 'But there must be some way we could manage. . .'

Rhona suddenly brightened, a crafty look in her face. 'I know of one way,' she burst out. '*You* could take Song out to Singapore with you and hand him over to Tang's sister. He'll be happy with her, she's been a second mother to him.'

'Couldn't you take him yourself?' Rosanna demurred, taken aback. 'I wasn't really intending going to Singapore.'

'No. You know I can't leave my job here until I've completed my six-month contract in surgery. Mr Gainsborough would be furious—you know how he is, and the strong line he takes against employing female doctors with children to bring up would put the kibosh on any hope of a good reference, to say nothing of his prejudice against deceptions! Maybe I've been foolish hiding the fact that I'm married and have a baby,' Rhona continued, growing increasingly troubled again, 'but I was warned about his strict views when I applied, so I knew he'd be dead set against giving me the appointment in surgery if he knew, but I just *had* to get it so that I could qualify for the job with Tang. I know *you* understood, Rosanna, but Stuart Gainsborough wouldn't have.'

'No, I agree there. I've never met anyone more unwaveringly against women combining the two jobs, mother and doctor,' said Rosanna.

'He might be a brilliant surgeon, but he's old-fashioned in that respect. . .simply won't accept that it's possible for a woman to make a success of both careers. If what I heard is true, his wife was a doctor, and look at the way she ruined his life, deserting their children and all that. . .perhaps that's what's affected him.' Rhona raised her shoulders despairingly. 'He probably bases his opinions of feminine capabilities on her, doesn't give the rest of us a chance to prove ourselves different. . .'

'I don't know anything about his private life,' Rosanna put in quickly, strangely loath to link another female with him. Then she hurriedly changed the course of the conversation.

CHAPTER THREE

'I'M AFRAID all my talk about the rights of children to have a stable home life with both parents couldn't have helped much when you were feeling as down as you were,' Rosanna remarked ruefully.

'No,' Rhona agreed. 'It made me thoroughly miserable. I felt I'd been selfish in keeping Song away from his father for so long, but there was no alternative as far as I could see.'

'Stuart Gainsborough's the real fly in the ointment.' Rosanna pulled a face, thinking of him. 'He's a hard man, quite intractable when it suits him. However, all isn't exactly gloom and doom. No one suspects the baby's yours. I've certainly never told anyone.'

'If I could just hang on until I get that reference— I'm nearly there. . .oh, Rosanna, what am I going to do?' sighed Rhona.

'You'd be prepared to let Song go to Singapore without you?'

'I haven't much choice in the matter.' Rhona sniffed and wiped an errant tear from her cheek. 'Especially now he's started having febrile convulsions whenever his temperature rises. He'd be better off with Tang's family than with someone with no medical knowledge or connections, that's another consideration.'

Lost in thought, Rosanna studied her hands. 'How long will it be before Song has his own passport?' she asked.

Hope began to shine in Rhona's eyes. 'It should be ready before your holiday starts.'

'And you say it would only be a very short time before you could join up with Song again?' Rosanna mused on, influenced by the enthusiastic acquiescence of Rhona's nods. 'But do you realise that in order to help you out I'd have to put up with Stuart's company for two full weeks? I honestly don't know that I could last out that long!'

'Especially as you'd have to keep up the pretence about Song not being mine.' Rhona became miserable again, realising the snags. 'Because if you were to give the game away I'd be more in the soup than ever. Mr Gainsborough wouldn't give me any reference at all, good, bad or indifferent!'

'I'm hopeless at acting or pretending,' Rosanna muttered. 'Fluffed the only line I was ever given to speak in a school play, so I'm bound to say the wrong thing to Stuart. Not that I'll mean to. Oh, why did the Armstrongs have to want to send Stuart with me to Singapore? Why couldn't they have flown him out to Timbuktu or somewhere, the farther away the better!'

Then she saw Rhona's crestfallen face.

'Oh, dear,' she put an arm around her, 'I'm being beastly, aren't I! You know, I hate myself sometimes! Of course I'll help you out, but don't expect me to do it without protest. You know me! I'm on edge, that's my trouble. Stuart's calling for me at eight to talk about the holiday. I was going to tell him straight out that I wouldn't go. How on earth do I deal with him now I've changed my mind?'

'You have?' Rhona immediately brightened. 'It's simple. Dress to kill. Build up your ego to match his, say only what you want to say. I'll understand if you do find you can't go through with the Singapore plan.' Her expression became touchingly noble.

Rosanna smiled pensively, knowing full well that she was caught in a trap of Rhona's making. Nevertheless she was fond of the girl and understood her problem. It was just a pity that to solve it she was left with no option but to go to Singapore with Stuart. . .and what was more, was faced with the onerous task of keeping him from guessing that little Song belonged to Rhona!

'It'll be good to have my mind put at ease,' Rhona sighed, this time with satisfaction. 'I'll be able to concentrate my energies on satisfactorily completing my surgery experience, that way I'm sure to earn a really good reference.'

Meanwhile I'll be the one doing all the dirty work, thought Rosanna a little resentfully. 'How will I keep Stuart from guessing about Song?' she asked out loud.

'He won't.' Rhona seemed to have it all thought out already. 'With Song being pronounced "Son" in the Singaporean way, Stuart will think you're calling him your son, so he'll suspect he's yours. After all, he doesn't know much about you, does he?'

And what annoyed Rosanna most was that she laughed as if it were all a great joke.

She herself was not so sure she would find the situation funny, but there was no time to say so, she had to hurry to get herself ready to go out with Stuart.

To her surprise he was a few minutes early in calling for her and arrived looked remarkably cheerful.

'Didn't you have any trouble finding my accommodation block?' she blurted out as she opened the door to him.

'No—why, was I mean to?' He gave her a quizzical glance, a knowing gleam in his eye.

Rosanna, darting back to take a last-minute look at her reflection in her dressing-table mirror while she put the final touches to the sophisticated hairstyle she had adopted for the evening, was glad he was unable to see her guilty blush.

She came out of her room to the accompaniment of a wolf-whistle so unexpected that she stopped short for a moment.

'Stunning and very feminine,' said Stuart, looking her up and down. 'You should always wear that striking contrast of blue and white. It brings out the pearly quality of your complexion.'

Coming from her room, Rhona winked at Rosanna behind his back, both girls knowing that make-up had a lot to do with it as well. Nevertheless Stuart's reaction to her new look gave Rosanna's spirits quite a lift. She was still a little bemused because of the wolf-whistle—something she had never ever expected to hear coming from Stuart Gainsborough!

He saw her into his car and whisked her away to a renowned little restaurant hidden away in a delightful little village of stone-built houses set in the heart of the wild but beautiful Lancashire Dales.

'You must be as hungry as I am,' he said, studying the menu after being shown to a table for two. 'What would you choose for starters? We'll eat first and talk later, shall we. . .anything to blot out the memory of that canteen sandwich!'

Rosanna studied him over the top of her tasselled menu card while he concentrated on selecting his own choice of dish.

With his brown hair brushed and shining, its slight wave subdued and his face more relaxed than she had ever seen it, he could almost be called handsome, she decided, adding the proviso that to give the best effect his deep-set eyes should remain half hooded to shade their intensity, losing their habitual frown, and his mouth should be allowed to soften. His lips were set far too severely straight. They needed to smile more easily.

'Well, what do you think of me?' he asked suddenly. 'I know you've been studying my face. I could feel myself being analysed feature by feature. Have I passed or failed the examination?'

To Rosanna's relief a young waitress made her appearance just then, coming to take their order, so she was spared the need to think up some uncompromising reply to give Stuart.

The meal was excellent, starting with a prawn cocktail and continuing with sea-bass with lemon and tagliatelle con panna e funghi, then Tournedos Rossini and fresh vegetables, before ending with strawberries and ice-cream.

All Rosanna wanted afterwards was to go to sleep, not to enter into a conversation, especially one which might well prove difficult. Her eyes kept closing even when she was out in the car with all the windows wide open letting in fresh air.

'I don't think it's much good talking to you tonight,' Stuart hinted after throwing several glances in her direction. 'You can rest your head on my shoulder and have a doze if you like,' he added.

'No, thank you.' Rosanna immediately sat bolt upright. 'I'm not a bit tired.' But in spite of her determination to resist the temptation, within minutes she was fast asleep and nestling against him, much to her discomfiture and embarrassment when he awakened her outside her front door.

'Thank you for the meal.' She managed to sound formally polite even if her steps were unsteady with the drowsiness still enveloping her even as she stepped out of the car.

'Get to bed.' He made it sound like an order. 'We'll talk tomorrow night, that's if you're awake enough.' Then he drove off.

'He isn't very understanding,' Rosanna complained to Rhona, collapsing on to the two-seater settee in the tiny lounge. 'He might have known I'd be too exhausted to be good company tonight. The dinner was delicious, but we hardly said a word to each other, he seemed to leave the talking to me and I wasn't up to it. And what do you think I did? Went to sleep against his shoulder when I got in the car, and after denying that I felt tired!'

Rhona, more wide awake than Rosanna, saw the funny side. 'He won't forget that in a hurry,' she laughed.

'Nor will I!' Rosanna dissolved into tired chuckles. 'He was quite abrupt with me afterwards, yet it was his idea really. He suggested I should put my head on his shoulder and have a doze. . .the thing is that I summerally. . .sumarilly. . .oh, dear, I can't think up the right word, I'm so sleepy still, anyway, what I'm trying to say is that I rejected the offer, then must have taken advantage of it almost immediately afterwards! He'll think me a fine one!'

'He's always nice to patients; maybe he'll put you in that category as you were so tired,' Rhona suggested consolingly.

'He has a *duty* to be nice to patients.' Rosanna sobered down. 'He won't care about *me*.' She shrugged. 'Duty first and foremost, that's his creed.'

'I think you're rather hard on him.'

'You think that because you make a point of seeing the best in everyone. I'm more cynical—not a nice person at all really.'

Rhona merely laughed.

'It's all right for you to laugh.' Rosanna remained serious. 'You'd be able to simply ignore Stuart's snide remarks and superiority tantrums, whereas I react badly to them. Two weeks with him will be a punishing experience for me. Instead of a holiday it'll be a penance!'

'I'm sorry I suggested it.' Rhona appeared crestfallen.

'Oh, don't take any notice of me, Rhona,' Rosanna said by way of apology. 'Something's got into me lately, and I don't know what it is—apart from exhaustion.'

Which was not strictly true. Rosanna knew very well

what was going on inside her. She was building up a love-hate relationship with Stuart Gainsborough, growing more attracted to him every day in spite of her resolve to ignore the feelings he aroused.

Attracted to him when she disliked everything about him. . .it was ironical and the very last thing she had wanted to happen, because life was complicated enough as it was.

Stuart Gainsborough. . .why, she didn't even like the man, or anything he stood for. Well, perhaps it wasn't right to say that, she admired his work as a surgeon, had to admit it was pretty brilliant. All the same, never to have seen him again would suit her very well. . .yet now she was committed to having to spend two whole weeks in his company! Was Rhona demanding more from her in friendship's name than she would be able to give?

She crept under her duvet that night, shivering as much as if winter had suddenly ousted the warmth of late summer.

The next morning Stuart was waiting for her in Casualty. 'I thought our A and E unit had netted a few extra thousands of pounds from the Department of Health's funding drive?' he queried. 'Wasn't that given for the express purpose of improving casualty services and to create a more homely and less daunting environment for children?' He surveyed the department with a critical eye. 'Well, I don't think much of your choice of new curtains, for a start.'

'What's wrong with them?' Rosanna was immediately on the defensive again, a triage nurse having edged her to the front of a gathering of casualty staff as if relying on her to stand up for them all and act on their behalf.

'Well, take another good look at those curtains. Can't you see how completely unsuitable they are for the children's waiting area? Women might like them, but they won't do a thing for youngsters!'

'You consider yourself an expert in these matters, Mr Gainsborough?'

Stuart ignored the sarcasm. 'And those pelmets!' He wrinkled up his aristocratic nose in distaste. 'Whose idea were those?'

Not mine, Rosanna wanted to say, but not for all the world was she going to hint that anyone else in the A and E unit was in any way at fault. She would far rather accept the undeserved blame herself if he wanted to make an issue of it. The sisters and nurses were her friends and treasured helpers.

'I thought surgery was your department, Mr Gainsborough,' she retorted. 'None of us would dream of criticising *your* choice of interior designs or decorations in theatre or on your wards.' Purposely, she too held her head high.

A few muffled sniggers came from a couple of student nurses standing behind her. Hearing them, Stuart stalked stiffly away from Casualty.

Everyone there breathed more freely.

'Is he sour because none of the extra funding is going to his theatre unit?' one of the nurses asked, adding an innocent, 'They do say they'll be having to make more cuts there if they don't get more money.'

'More cuts in surgery!' another of the nurses quipped. 'How very appropriate!'

Everyone burst out laughing then, and Rosanna sighed with relief, glad the atmosphere had been restored to its usual friendly liveliness.

She was waylaid by Stuart, however, when she was on her way up the stairs to see a patient she had had referred to the orthopaedic ward.

'Could you stay awake long enough this evening to discuss this holiday business?' he asked abruptly. 'It's important that we should decide on a plan of action without further delay.'

'I thought it was being decided for us,' she remarked.

'And you'd be content with that? Personally I like to make my own arrangements,' he said, sounding vexed.

'Well, so do I, usually.'

'But this time you aren't sufficiently keen on the proposed holiday to take much interest in it. Is that what you mean?'

'If you like to think so.' Rosanna, irritated by his manner, stood her ground. 'But now I have work to do for a patient. You'll have to excuse me.' She tried to walk on past him.

'I'm calling for you at seven,' he declared decisively, staying her by putting a hand on her arm.

Involuntarily she stared down at it, then gazed up at him, her eyes startled. For his part Stuart was looking equally disturbed. Then, after what seemed like an earth-stopping moment, his hand—fisting with tension—dropped away from her and instead dug deep into his white coat pocket.

'Tonight,' he insisted, regaining his composure. 'Be ready.' Then he walked off, his long strides more purposeful than ever, his head held high.

Rosanna took a deep breath to help steady her heart. She studied her wristwatch. How long a wait was it until seven? she wondered, as if it mattered, then chided herself because somehow it did. It mattered very much, and she didn't know why.

'Are you still wanting me to take Song to Singapore?' she asked Rhona after work finished for the day and the two girls were getting ready to go out, Rhona to be with her baby, and Rosanna to accompany Stuart.

'Why, have you changed your mind?' Rhona questioned anxiously.

'I haven't really made it up yet. The only reason I'd go with Stuart would be for your sake. He's having a peculiar effect on me and I don't like it, I don't like it at all.'

'You're not falling for him, are you?'

'Oh, Rhona, how could you even hint at such a thing!' Rosanna protested, brushing her short ash-blonde hair ever more vigorously and until it had a silk-like sheen. 'He's so pompous, and he's only thirty-four. What's he going to be like when he's a senior consultant and even more able to throw his weight about? I'm sorry for him more than anything—yes, that's it. I pity him his future, he's going to be so disliked, even more so than now.'

'Some of the nurses and female physios don't seem to find him at all dislikable,' Rhona pointed out. 'Rather the opposite. . .even his secretary, Alexa, is quite besotted. They all buzz around him like bees around. . .'

'Don't name a flower,' Rosanna begged sourly, 'or I'll die laughing. Stinging nettles would be more apt, that's if bees like nettles? I wouldn't know.' She paused, suddenly wrapped in nostalgia. 'I suppose that's because with all the necessary reading and medical training I never had time to study them in our garden when I lived at home. The humming of bees among the flowers in our English country garden. . .oh well, just another of the many things I missed out on, I suppose.'

She stopped talking, determinedly blinking unbidden tears away. And now without Dad and Mother there simply isn't any home or garden, there's only accommodation, she had been about to add, but the words hurt too much, were too sad to say.

Rhona knew her well enough, however, to guess at her unhappy thoughts. 'You need a break,' she said perceptively. 'Apart from helping me out with Song, I think the complete change of scenery and different way of life will do you a world of good, Stuart or no Stuart.

Make use of him—you'll need a man to escort you around Singapore, and he'll suit that purpose if nothing else.'

'You'd better not let him hear you say so,' warned Rosanna, bracing herself. 'He's at the front door now, I think. Yes, listen. . .would anybody else ring the bell as imperatively, almost as if summoning a butler or footman and expecting to be formally announced?'

Chuckling, Rhona disappeared into her own bedroom, leaving Rosanna to open the door to him.

CHAPTER FOUR

'Good, you're ready,' said Stuart. 'I won't come in, I'll go and wait in the car.'

Rosanna had never seen him in casual wear before. His well-tailored trousers and Aran sweater greatly enhanced his appearance, she thought as she followed him out to his Mercedes convertible.

'Why stare at me?' he asked, stepping over the door into the open-topped car, sitting down and stretching out his long legs towards the pedals.

'You look so different.' Rosanna settled herself in the passenger seat. 'Such a change from those ghastly theatre greens. . .'

'With the trousers held up by string because the waist sizes would fit Tweedledum and Tweedledee laced together?'

Rosanna laughed with him, then stopped, surprised at herself for actually finding anything to laugh at while she was with Stuart. Adding to her embarrassment, he caught hold of her hand, placed it on the gear lever, and covered it with his own.

Although for some reason she failed to understand, her heart leapt at the touch of his fingers, nevertheless she resisted the temptation to let her hand remain under his and instead drew it away, reminding herself crossly that he had been holding it without so much as a 'by your leave' just when she had had no intention whatsoever of encouraging him.

'Where shall we eat?' he asked, inexplicably vexing her even more by making no attempt to repossess her hand. 'Any suggestions?'

'It depends on whether you want a proper meal or

not.' At the prospect of food Rosanna put all other considerations aside. She was very hungry, not having had time to have more than tea and a slice or two of toast since getting up that morning. Hoping to hear he was equally famished, she actually asked him.

'I always need a meal when I come off duty,' he replied. 'I expect you do too. In the old days we used to be able to pay for something hot and substantial to be sent along to us in Theatre, but now Admin finds it cheaper to supply packet soup and a roll free rather than pay kitchen staff to stay on and cook. Do you fare as badly?'

'Worse. We don't even get the offer of soup! The nurses take pity on us and provide tea and toast when they can, but they're kept very busy too, even if they do get an official lunch or tea break—which is more than we doctors can lay claim to!'

'We think ourselves very hard done by, don't we?' Stuart commented drily. 'Brings to mind all those starving millions who *can't* drive out to pubs and hotels for a good meal!' He glanced towards Rosanna. 'Same place as last time,' he suggested, 'or was that too inducive to sleep?'

First he chastises, then he teases, thought Rosanna, aggrieved yet unable to stop a blush at the memory of how she had nestled against his shoulder on that previous occasion. For how long? she wondered, having no way of knowing, then she remembered being quite shaken at the lateness of the hour when she returned to the flat. She must have slept very soundly. She only hoped she hadn't snored!

Hastily she suggested they should try the Golden Eagle Hotel in a nearby village. 'I'm told that the views from the windows are really worth seeing,' she added as an inducement.

'Oh, it isn't just that the meals might be lighter there?' The taunting note was back in Stuart's voice.

Rosanna sighed, deeply this time.

'Oh, I'm sorry,' he gave her a shrewd look, 'I do tend to take the mickey, don't I! Am I spoiling the Dales for you? You love them, don't you. . .well, so do I, believe it or not.'

Rosanna decided to go along with his new mood. 'The mountainous roads are so astonishingly majestic in their rugged beauty,' she said appreciatively. 'I love the wildness, the spaciousness, the tumbling waterfalls. . .'

'And the lack of traffic?' There was a hint of a smile in his voice. He stopped the car, twisted round to face her and put an arm behind her shoulders.

Her heart beating fast, she waited wonderingly.

'It's all right,' his voice was strangely gruff in spite of the reassurance of his words, 'I'm only reaching over to the map pocket in the door beside you. I'm not going to molest you. I don't know this Golden Eagle Hotel you mentioned. Do *you* know the way to it?'

They studied the map together, Rosanna very conscious of his nearness. Fearing a shy nervous tremor in her voice might betray her wayward emotions, she refrained from saying anything at all, waiting instead for him to move away so that she could gather her senses about her and allow her feelings to settle. At the moment they were definitely topsy-turvy, confused, anything but stable, and she was most annoyed with herself because she seemed to have so little control over them.

'How's Peter Armstrong getting on?' Finally she forced herself to speak if only to remind Stuart of the reason for their being together. 'I haven't been up to see him just recently,' she explained.

'I know. He was complaining about that to me. It seems the only reason he wants to stay in hospital is to have the chance of seeing you.' Stuart folded the map away.

'Well, I think I know how to get to the hotel,' he added, starting up the car again. 'It's probably further on than you remembered, however—either that or I've been going around in circles getting nowhere.' He paused, to add wryly, 'I seem to have a habit of doing that where you're concerned, Rosanna.'

She turned her head away, not wanting him to see her colour rise—as it did, it seemed to her, whenever he made any sort of personal remark.

He said nothing more, however, simply driving on through enchanting hamlets of pretty cottages, their delightful hanging baskets of flowers drawing the eye to the attractive stone-built walls and the immaculate net curtains at the windows.

Finally, after skilfully negotiating more narrow, twisting and very hilly roads, he parked the Mercedes in the forecourt of the Golden Eagle Hotel.

Sitting comfortably in the lounge while waiting for a table, Rosanna enthused over the landscape of high peaks and wooded gills disturbed only by frothy white streaks of waterfalls forcing a way down through heathers and fronds of fern.

'And in summer pale mauve foxgloves and purple saxifrages vie with buttercups, daisies, tiny birds' eye primulas and wild orchids especially to delight our senses,' she sighed dreamily. 'I do think we've a lot to be thankful for in having been given so much beauty to enjoy—all for free too!'

'Your grammar leaves much to be desired at times,' Stuart rebuked her, although laughter-lines she had never noticed before crinkled the corners of his eyes. 'No one would think you a gifted and learned surgeon. . .a Fellow of the Royal College!'

'Gifted and learned is a description which hardly applies to me, although the brains to do the necessary studying must certainly have been a gift, I couldn't have manufactured them myself, but as for 'learned'—

well, using them I merely passed the necessary exams, so to God goes the credit.'

'You mustn't take everything I say quite so seriously. I'm told I have a dry sense of humour, whatever that implies,' said Stuart. 'Anyway, to change the subject completely, I just want to say that next time we'll try and come earlier. The countryside colours are becoming muted in the fading light of evening—although perhaps your imagination enables you to see everything clothed in its true glory even now?'

Ignoring the rest of his words, Rosanna noted only that he obviously intended there to be a 'next time'. The thought filled her with a surprising gladness. Not that she would necessarily agree to accompany him again, she promised herself hastily, but it would be nice to be asked.

Then she noticed he was looking at her and not at the views from the windows.

'I see you're wearing blue and white again.' He nodded approvingly. 'Is that because I expressed my admiration of your choice of colours last time?'

'Of course not,' Rosanna denied hotly, forcibly drawing herself back to reality. 'This dress happened to be the only one already ironed, and you didn't leave me much time to prepare anything else.'

'How mundane,' he muttered, sounding disappointed. 'And I thought you were making a special effort to please me!'

'Why should I?' she returned perkily. 'Anyway, *I* thought we were here to discuss the Singapore affair?'

'Is that what you call it? An affair. . .as in *affaire de coeur*? Well, that's better, I was beginning to despair of ever breaking through that brittle shell you call a heart.'

He's teasing me yet again, Rosanna thought vexedly, taking a quick peep at him and fancying amusement quirked the corner of his mouth.

'You know what I mean,' she claimed primly, defying another blush to give her away as he followed her to a table and sat down opposite her.

'What are you going to have?' he asked, handing her the menu. 'Smoked salmon, side salad, thin brown bread and butter? That should be a light enough meal to keep you awake.'

Rosanna smiled. It was going to be fun if Stuart remained as light-hearted and considerate for the whole of the coming holiday. But could he? A shadow crossed her face. What when he found out she was aiming to make use of him, keeping up Rhona's pretence? What a mess everything would be then!

'Don't look so worried, frowns don't suit faces like yours.' He shone the table lamp towards her. 'Turn up the corners of that pretty mouth.' With a gentle finger he traced a smile over her lips as if sketching it on.

Rosanna drew back out of his reach.

'You've gone cold on me again,' he said, his own smile dying. 'Honestly, I find you the most enigmatic young woman I've ever known! I can't understand you at all. You're certainly not the easiest of companions. Do you think we'll be able to stay friends long enough to enjoy Singapore together?'

Rosanna's expression showed she seriously doubted it, but that was because her conscience was plaguing her more and more every minute. It was difficult having to keep Rhona's secret all the time it was necessary to do so, but what of the future? How would Stuart react to finding out that he had been made a pawn in his SHO's ladder-climbing career. . .and that she, Rosanna, had encouraged and helped to this end?

He would be angry, justifiably so. . .but what could she do about it at this late stage? She had had no wish to cheat him or anyone.

She should never have let the matter get so far. Yet she was fond of Rhona and understood her quandary, knowing she would be heartbroken now if her carefully laid plans went awry.

Besides, baby Song needed to be looked after, and who better to do it than his own father and family? Filled with worry, Rosanna left most of her food untouched.

'Are you all right?' asked Stuart. 'Not feeling sick or anything. . .only you're not eating and you've hardly said a word. . . This holiday business, is it worrying you? Would you rather not come?'

'Oh, but I must!' Rosanna was startled into making it sound imperative that she should.

'There's no must about it—I'm sure the Armstrongs would allow one of the nurses to take your place if you'd rather not come. Perhaps even my secretary would oblige?'

'Oh, no, that won't be necessary!' Rosanna bristled at the very thought of the glamorous Alexa having Stuart all to herself.

Stuart brightened. 'So in spite of tonight's puzzling performance you're really keen to accompany me? That's great. I'd begun to fear. . .well, never mind what I'd begun to fear.'

They spent the next hour or two talking about the trip and the arrangements to be made, Rosanna carefully refraining from mentioning Song.

But when she went to bed that night she cried, knowing it was unlikely that Stuart would ever forgive her for what he would see as intolerable deceit on her part.

However, when over their breakfast of tea and toast in the morning Rhona was so grateful and in such high spirits, Rosanna knew she had no alternative but to keep her promise and help Rhona out.

'Song's already had all the necessary inoculations,' Rhona told her jubilantly. 'No problem there. And I've seen to his passport and the essential documen-

tation, it's all being processed, and Tang's making sure
everything's in order at the Singapore end. His sister's
eager to take over with Song again, and their father's
making a good recovery from his stroke, so everything's hunky-dory! Tang phoned last night when you
were out. Did you enjoy yourself with Stuart?'

'So-so.' Rosanna could only manage a half-smile.

'This holiday in Singapore will give you a chance to
really get to know him. I think he quite likes you,' said
Rhona.

Rosanna got up from the table. 'Well, he won't like
me for long.' She pulled a wry face. 'Not that I care,'
she added, as much to convince herself as to convince
Rhona.

Then she hurried over to the hospital, hoping she
would see him, yet when she did catch a glimpse of
him coming towards her along the corridor she almost
panicked, turning tail and hurrying away in a direction
she had no real need to go.

'You disappeared as rapidly as a scared rabbit when
you saw me this morning,' he commented when he was
called to Casualty to give a second opinion on a
particularly complicated injury which might or might
not necessitate surgery. 'Do I really have such a drastic
effect on your emotions, Rosanna?'

'*Is* an operation needed?' Purposely she drew his
mind back to the job in hand.

'On you?' Facetiously he deliberated. 'Well, I'm no
brain surgeon. . .but hearts? Now *those* are my special-
ity. When would you like yours opened up a little?'

'I'm being serious,' Rosanna chided, trying to look
severe and earnest and at least twice her age. 'What
about the patient?'

'He'll be fine.' Stuart's immediate sober pro-
fessionalism matched hers. 'Keep him in under observation if you're worried about him, but I don't think
you need be. I've seen accidental injuries like his

before and they've responded to treatment without surgical help being involved. Do you feel like coming out for a meal again tonight?'

'No, thank you,' was Rosanna's cool response to his seemingly impulsive invitation, but as he strode away back to his surgical ward she wondered why she had refused him when all she had wanted since awakening that morning was to be with him again.

It continued to be a frustrating day. She was due to give an early morning talk, with prepared slides, to the consultant and the new casualty officers, but when she went along to the lecture-room it was already occupied.

'Have you ordered breakfast?' she asked the consultant, her nose in the air sniffing the appetising odour of bacon, sausages, mushrooms, tomatoes and scrambled eggs accompanied by coffee and toast.

'No, not me,' Mr Hurst replied, 'but look, what's this?' Hurriedly sidestepping, he moved out of the way of a food-laden trolley, then, his face wreathed in happy anticipation, 'I guess all this food must have been provided courtesy of a drug rep,' he remarked, winking at her. 'I think we'll be doing more eating than meeting!'

Laughing, Rosanna sat with him and the SHOs to enjoy more breakfast than she had eaten in years, the drug representative taking the opportunity to show an educational video to his happy captive audience, rewarding their attention with a generous distribution of pens and slimline torches all tactfully advertising the drug he was trying to promote.

'Give the talk tomorrow instead of today,' suggested Mr Hurst to Rosanna afterwards, leaving her to take his clinic for him while he did a ward round.

The new SHOs gathered around her, all anxious to learn, not having done any casualty work before, since they had just completed their first year as housemen—

housemen not being allowed to work as casualty officers.

'Normally I revel in teaching,' Rosanna said to Rhona that evening. 'But today the large breakfast blunted my appetite for coaching. Reducing a fracture under Bier's block with a dozen enquiring eyes watching was quite a strain, so too was the removal of a foreign body from a child's ear.'

'What foreign body?'

Rosanna laughed. 'A tablet. The child had been told the tablets were given to make her ear better, so naturally she put one in her ear, thinking it would do the trick! Just shows how careful one has to be when explaining things to children, doesn't it?'

'I heard you had an RTA to contend with too?'

'Yes, a mother and three children were involved. "Mummy skidded and a naughty car came across and hit us," sobbed the five-year-old, although I think the mother thought herself to blame for the accident. Most drivers do, don't they—at first, anyway, until they're warned by their insurance companies not to commit themselves! Anyway, no great harm was done to our threesome. The mother's being kept in overnight, but the father was able to take the children home pretty well straight away.'

'In Theatre Stuart was cross because of you taking the metal from that industrial worker's knee, he said it should have been done under general anaesthetic,' Rhona remarked.

'Didn't need to be,' Rosanna declared stalwartly. 'I managed perfectly well with just a local and the patient was able to go back to work, much to his relief. He'd have lost a day's pay if Stuart had had his way.'

Rhona topped up their mugs with fresh coffee. 'What happened in your Area Three? I heard that there was blood everywhere!'

'So there was. A patient had been passing blood but

also had heart trouble, so he was referred to the medics. One came, but didn't want to put in blood because of the heart's condition. Then the patient collapsed, the heart beating only eighteen per minute. Having to act quickly, the physician pumped up the pressure bag, but he pumped too high and it exploded. Blood went everywhere, all over Mr Hurst, it even ran over and under the curtains to the next-door patient—who, poor woman, almost had a fit!'

'Blood from the bag, you mean?' queried Rhona.

'Oh, yes, so it didn't really matter. Both patients are all right now, but it was a gory experience. Mr Hurst stumbled out from the cubicle with a large syringe in his hand and his spectacles dripping blood, the red stuff all over his shirt and hands. Talk about a horror movie! I don't know what the people in the waiting area must have thought; most of them left in a hurry!'

'What a catastrophe!' Rhona tried to keep a straight face, but when she and Rosanna looked at each other, each mentally conjuring up a picture of the horrific scene, fully realising the terror the bloodstained consultant must have put in the hearts of the waiting patients, they just couldn't restrain their giggles until, sides aching, they went to bed.

CHAPTER FIVE

FROM the beginning of the school holidays the Casualty Department filled more rapidly every day. Children were brought in one after another with injuries caused by falling off swings, ropes, bikes, slides, climbing frames, skate-boards, or anything else they could tumble from, besides collecting more squashed fingers than the Casualty staff could count.

'And now of course it's wasp-sting time—you'd be surprised how many people get stung. There was a child the other day who was eating a jam sandwich on the beach when a wasp stung her tongue, poor kid. She's OK now, but she would have been saved a lot of pain had she been able to receive medical attention earlier. It wasn't our fault, she wasn't brought in soon enough. Her parents said they were waiting until she was well enough to visit her GP. . . I ask you!'

Rosanna looked around the group of SHOs she was tutoring about the best methods of dealing with various ailments. 'It's strange really, because most patients are brought to us instead of to their local GPs,' she reflected. 'I can't think why. We could do with being left to see to the more seriously hurt, that way we'd be able to reduce the waiting time and considerably shorten our lists—much to everyone's satisfaction.'

'What *do* we do for wasp-stings?' asked one of the newest of the casualty officers.

'Well, it depends. A lot of swelling would indicate an allergy, so one would use an anti-histamine like Terfenadine, but in that case the patient would have to be warned not to drive or use machinery, as drowsiness could be an effect of the drug. If the sting's infected, use antibiotics.'

'But if it's just a perfectly normal sting?'

'Oh, in that event simply apply vinegar or lemon, something acidic, even a slice of onion perhaps if that's handiest. Some of the old remedies are still the most helpful. . .applying ice to cool down inflammation, for instance. Nowadays one could keep a small bag of peas in the deep-freeze ready for just such an eventuality. They can prove very effective when placed over the inflammation, believe me. I've experienced for myself the relief they can bring when needed.'

'You've got a visitor, Rosanna,' Sister Mills put her head around the corner to announce. 'I showed him into the eye-room, as all the cubicles were occupied.'

'A visitor?' Rosanna was puzzled. She rarely had visitors, so as soon as she could she hurried along to the eye-room.

Peter Armstrong was sitting in the patients' chair facing the eye-test chart, his head leaning back against the chair's headrest, his feet propped up on the splay legs of the lamp standing by the trolley.

'If you want your eyes irrigated, lie down,' Rosanna greeted him jocularly, 'or is this simply a social visit?'

'It's more than that.' Peter flinched with the pain of stretching his sore ribs while attempting to get to his feet. 'It's a personal request,' he explained fractiously. 'A do-or-die plea, so it's no laughing matter.'

'Stay sitting,' Rosanna commanded in the official voice she reserved for awkward patients, suspicions rising to convince her that Peter was not going to be easy to deal with. She perched herself on the edge of the trolley, facing him. 'Just tell me what the trouble is. I've got many patients to see to, so please don't be offended if I hurry you.'

'I want to go to Singapore with you,' Peter declared sullenly. 'I don't want you to go with Stuart

Gainsborough. I want to be the one to personally witness your first reaction to everything you see, to experience it all with you, and only you. So will you get him to take someone else while you wait until *I* can travel with you?' You'd still go all expenses paid, I promise you.'

His face was pale and strained, and Rosanna felt a little worried about him. 'You should be resting at home, Peter—please go back now,' she urged.

'I had to come or there wouldn't have been time for a change of plan.'

She could see he was in deadly earnest. 'Look, Peter,' she responded, equally seriously, 'There's something you don't know—a crucial reason why I have to get to Singapore as quickly as possible. I wish I could tell you more, but I must get back to my work right now. Please trust me. I'd wait and go with you if I could, but I'd be letting someone down very badly if I did, and I don't want to do that.'

'Mr Gainsborough isn't the only person in love with you,' Peter muttered petulantly.

Rosanna's heart overturned at his assumption concerning Stuart. 'Mr Gainsborough is not in love with me,' she denied vehemently, sliding down from the trolley. 'And the reason I have to go to Singapore so soon has nothing to do with him. Now I simply must go round to the front of A and E and see more patients. I'll get a porter to see you to your car. I presume you came by car?'

'Yes. The chauffeur parked just outside the main entrance.' Peter looked and sounded sorry for himself. 'Don't be angry with me, Rosanna,' he added in a hangdog way. 'I guess I'm just rather jealous, that's all, and you can't really blame me, can you?' He reached for her hand and kissed it. 'You've stolen my heart, you know, I've been dreaming of you night and day. If I send the car for you some time will you come and see me?'

'Of course,' Rosanna agreed, pitying him and not even guessing at the trouble he was going to cause in the future. 'Just ring me first,' she added as an afterthought.

'He's sending for me tomorrow evening,' she told Rhona after receiving Peter's phone call that evening. 'The question is, do I tell him about Song, or would you rather I didn't? He doesn't understand why I won't postpone my trip to Singapore so that he can accompany me. If I can't supply a good reason he's going to get very hurt, I can see that coming. And he's in no fit state to have mental strain to battle against as well as all his physical wounds.'

'Do you think you can trust him not to tell anyone else?' asked Rhona.

Rosanna shrugged her shoulders. 'I don't know. I just don't know.'

'Then don't risk it,' urged Rhona. 'It'll be catastrophic for me if he spills the beans before I finish here.'

'I know, so I won't tell him until you have Stuart's reference safely in your pocket, but keeping your secret isn't going to be easy.' The worry lines on Rosanna's forehead deepened.

But the next evening there was a pile-up on the motorway involving eight cars and, in all, twenty passengers. Rosanna was needed to help supervise the treatment of the injured.

Losing no time, she travelled out in the hospital's emergency ambulance, Eagle Two, doing what she could to help on the spot before accompanying the worst affected to the hospital, then sorting them out to the various wards according to their needs.

There was no option but to have a message phoned to Peter cancelling her visit. 'I don't see how I can possibly spare time to see him now that the trip to Singapore looms so high on the horizon,' she said to Rhona when she finally finished for the night. 'There's so much to see to, plus wanting to spend every spare minute I can with little Song so that he'll be happy with me on the flight.'

'Which *is* rather essential,' agreed Rhona. 'I wouldn't like him to react to you as he does to strangers, and you haven't been able to be with him all that much just lately.'

'In any case, I don't want to encourage Peter,' Rosanna added thoughtfully, her face very serious.

'You don't like him? You prefer Stuart?'

'I'm not prepared to form a romantic relationship with anyone at the moment.' Rosanna lowered her eyes, not wanting Rhona to see the secret longing which crept into them whenever Stuart's name was mentioned, especially when and if her innermost feelings about him were suddenly left open to scrutiny.

'However,' continued Rhona, not appearing to have noticed Rosanna's unwillingness to discuss Stuart, 'you won't be able to avoid Peter when you actually leave for the airport. Isn't he insisting on taking you there in the family limousine to see you off?'

'Yes, unfortunately. I'd rather have gone under my own steam, but as his father's the generous donor of the holiday I didn't see how I could refuse.'

Yet if she had not been so concerned about the outcome of Peter's first meeting with Song when he called to pick her up, she might have found it impossible not to be amused by his startled gape when he saw her with a child in her arms.

'Can you keep a secret?' she had asked instead without preamble, hurrying out to the car. 'This is Song, and I don't want anyone in the hospital to know about him. I'm taking him to his father. He's been pretty well hidden until now because some consultants

are so against women trying to combine motherhood
with the practice of medicine that they refuse to give
them good references to help promote them into other
jobs when the time comes for them to move on to their
next six months' training post.'

Breathless after gabbling the explanation she was far
from happy about, she eyed him dubiously, wondering
if he understood, because in spite of having rehearsed
over and over again before he arrived, she knew she
was making a mess of all she had meant to say and the
way she had planned to say it.

The determination to keep Rhona's secret had
caused her carefully prepared words to stumble over
each other unconvincingly, making little sense, she
thought.

'I understand,' said Peter, although remaining
obviously perplexed. 'The time has come for you to
move on to another hospital, and although you're
married to Stuart Gainsborough and this is your child
you haven't told him about it? Surely it's a most
extraordinary way to behave?' He paused, to continue
glumly after a moment or two. 'I didn't know you and
he were married!'

'We're not—you've got it all wrong. Look, we're at
the airport already. Stuart's going to have a shock.'

'I'll say!' Peter glanced pointedly at little Song.

Rosanna shrugged, giving up on the effort to get him
to understand even a little. 'Come on,' she urged. 'I
can see him over there—let's dodge him!'

And holding Song tightly to her, she stepped down
from the car, then waited, realising Peter was not
altogether over his operation so could only move
comparatively slowly.

'You're not at all the person I thought you were,'
Peter muttered, 'or you'd never have acted like this.
Tell Stuart the truth, Rosanna.'

She covered Song's head with his shawl, hoping to

hide him a while longer. 'No, no, that's the one thing I mustn't do,' she maintained heatedly. 'I promised I wouldn't. Oh, Peter, I must rush. Look, get a porter to stick those cases on a trolley—I'll manage the hand luggage. I've got to leave you now. Please have faith in me. I'll explain everything when I get back, I promise.'

Looking wildly around to check on the wherabouts of Stuart, growing desperate to board the plane before he could see Song, she was too late to stop Peter's arms going around her, too late too to avoid the passionate kiss he planted on her surprised lips.

'You shouldn't have done that!' she cried, instant tears of dismay springing from her eyes to run down her cheeks as she caught sight of Stuart watching from the back of a queue of waiting passengers.

'Why not?' Peter asked belligerently. 'From what you've told me you must be pretty lavish with your favours, so why shouldn't I have a share? You know how I feel about you. . .'

'Don't speak so loudly, people will hear you,' she demurred, distressed. 'You're completely misunderstanding the whole situation, and I haven't time to explain further. Just trust me, Peter—there's really nothing wrong in what I'm doing. I'll be telling Stuart all he needs to know. Oh dear, we're disturbing little Song, he's waking up. . . I've got to go. . .hush, Song, hush. . .'

As usual she pronounced Song like 'son'—the way Rhona had insisted she must because it was the way his father and all the Singaporean in-laws, including Nimi, the aunt who had been looking after him, said it. But Peter, listening, felt his suspicions had been confirmed.

'So he *is* your son!' he declared, piqued. 'Why all the secrecy? You don't want Stuart to know you're married, is that it? But what about when you hand the child over to your husband, won't his suspicions be aroused then?'

'I haven't got a husband.' Agitatedly Rosanna looked around the departure hall, desperate not to be seen by Stuart.

'Song *must* go to his father,' she explained distractedly. 'There's no one to leave him with otherwise, and he isn't well. I just don't want Stuart to see him yet, not until we're safely on the plane, in case he makes a fuss and refuses to accompany us.'

Her grey eyes misting appealingly, she turned back to Peter.

'I know I can't expect you to understand all that's happening, it's so complicated and I haven't time to explain, but couldn't you *please* just keep Stuart occupied until I've had time to board the plane?'

She beseeched so charmingly that anyone who had a heart would have been won over, and Peter was no exception. He looked at her adoringly, so she carried on with her attempt at persuasion.

'Your father will be so disappointed if we don't have this holiday he's arranged for our benefit,' she added for good measure, 'yet Stuart won't go if he knows I'm taking the child with me. It's only for the journey—I shan't have him with me afterwards. Oh, look, here comes Stuart—*please* don't let him see us. . .help me, Peter, just this once. . . I'll make it up to you when I come back.'

Peter's eyes brightened. 'That's a firm promise?'

'Of course.' Rosanna knew she had said the wrong thing immediately the words were out. Peter would hold her to her word, and that could make for problems. Nevertheless she had to get on the plane before Stuart, and if Peter engineered that—well, at least it would be something. It was no good wasting time worrying about what Peter might expect of her in the future.

Breaking away from him, she hid herself among the passengers waiting by the semi-automated baggage handling system until she remembered Mr Armstrong saying he intended booking Stuart and herself into the business class of the Singapore plane, thus entitling them to extra facilities such as using a special check-in counter, and giving them baggage priority.

Would Stuart remember? If so she would stand little chance of getting along to the Singapore airliner before him.

Pulling Song's shawl even further over his head to hide him as best she could, she hastily cast a cautious glance over her shoulder.

Stuart had his back to her. His height made him stand out above the crowd. Peter was shorter, she could see only the top of his handsome head, but the two men were talking together. Obviously Peter was detaining Stuart as she had asked.

She shuddered a little, remembering the look in Peter's eye and knowing there would be a price to pay when she returned. However, once again she cast the worry from her. Other things were going smoothly, she reminded herself. No one had queried her about Song's passport, and providing he sat on her lap and didn't occupy a seat, he didn't need a ticket—Rhona had been right about that too. And people with small children were allowed to board first, she found to her relief.

Finally boarding the plane, her arms aching from carrying sturdy little Song as well as the hand lugggage, she sank thankfully down on to the wide seat allotted to her by a smiling stewardess.

Stretching out, taking advantage of the extra leg-room provided in the business section of the plane, she rested, Song happily riding her knees.

Fully awake now, he stared around, his very dark eyes round with wonder at the strangeness of every-thing. Delighted to have succeeded in getting him aboard without Stuart's knowledge, Rosanna jogged him up and down playfully, rewarded by his happy chuckles.

'Who's this cheerful little fellow?' asked Stuart, arriving at last and taking the seat beside her. 'I presume you're baby-sitting for one of the passengers?'

So Peter hasn't told him anything, Rosanna thought thankfully, while to Stuart she said merely, 'No, he's travelling with me, aren't you, Song?'

Just as misled as Peter had been by her pronunciation of Song as 'son'. . . 'He's yours? Surely not!' Stuart's voice grew abrasive suddenly. 'Peter Armstrong told me I was in for a shock, but I didn't expect anything like this!'

Startled and distressed by the anger in the unfamiliar male voice, Song started to cry. Then the take-off procedure alarmed him even more. There was no pacifying him after that. Every few seconds he would turn his face from where he had it buried against Rosanna's chest, take another baleful peep at Stuart and start bawling louder than ever.

'He has a fine pair of lungs, I'll say that for him.' Stuart eyed him disapprovingly, at which—as if considering himself scolded—Song pouted out his lower lip, then, chin quivering, opened his mouth wide and nearly brought down the plane's roof with his mighty howls of protest.

The businessmen in the seats in front rustled their papers vexedly, coughed irritably, scowled meaningly, until finally Rosanna called one of the cabin crew specially assigned to the business class and asked whether she could be found another seat farther away where Song's cries would not be such a nuisance to others nor cause such a commotion.

Obligingly she was housed in the first-class section where, as it so happened, there was plenty of spare room.

'Shall I move too?' Stuart prepared to carry her hand luggage for her.

'No fear!' Rosanna hurriedly put out a hand to push him back into his seat. 'The poor boy's scared stiff of you—please just keep away.'

'But I wanted to talk to you,' he groused as she gathered up her possessions. Song quietened down as he realised they were moving away from the big stranger he found such a threat.

'This is a fine how d'you do,' Stuart went on muttering half to himself, frowning resentfully. 'You've been very secretive. I didn't know you were married.'

'I'm not,' Rosanna sighed, dreading another argument and beginning to move away.

'Divorced, then?'

'I don't believe in divorce.' She marched off with Song writhing impatiently in her arms, causing her to drop some of the hastily repacked requisites from her hand luggage.

As if trying to make sense of Rosanna's answers to his questions Stuart sat reflecting for a moment or two without moving, but one of the businessmen got up and followed her, picking up all she dropped and carefully laying the things beside her when she sat down in the first-class area.

Deciding that hunger might be a contributory cause of Song's distress, Rosanna lost no time in feeding him from one of the bottles Rhona had prepared, then, after burping him, changed his nappy in the tiny room set aside for the convenience of mothers and babies.

With the satisfaction of knowing she had made him as comfortable as possible she sat back in her seat nursing him, rocking him gently to and fro in the hope that he would go off into a sound sleep. She was feeling pretty exhausted herself after the early busy and very exhausting start to the day.

Very soon his eyes closed. With nothing else to do

Rosanna sat staring out of the little window beside her until even the fascination of the wonderful platform of various cloud formations failed to keep her from falling asleep herself and she nodded off, her cheek cushioned on the thick dark curls gracing the top of the child's sleepy head.

Awakening some hours later, she found Stuart occupying the formerly empty seat beside her. He too was asleep.

She studied his face, thinking how different it looked in repose, the lines of strain gone, the stern mouth relaxed. There was an endearing youthfulness showing through, a characteristic which she would never before have believed existed.

Slowly he opened one eye. 'Is it time to wake up?' he asked. 'Are we about to land?'

'You think we're on Concorde?' Rosanna quipped.

He stayed serious, stretching lazily. 'I had to come here to be with you,' he said. 'That chap who picked up your belongings would have taken the seat beside you if I hadn't beaten him to it. There was a certain look in his eye.'

'I'm surprised you recognised it,' Rosanna said impishly, 'I've never seen as much as a romantic gleam in yours!'

'Huh,' growled Stuart. 'I'm as human as the next man, but I don't believe in showing my feelings to all and sundry.' He looked down at Song and frowned. 'Is the boy all right?' he queried. 'It looks to me as if he's running a bit of a temperature.'

'Oh no!' Rosanna felt Song's forehead. 'You're right,' she agreed, dismayed. 'He's decidedly clammy. He did have a slight cold recently, and he does tend to get febrile convulsions when he's out of sorts or his temperature rises. Here, hold him for a minute, will you. . .'

'He'll scream!' Pretending cowardice, Stuart tried to

edge away, but Rosanna took no notice, planting Song firmly in his lap while she sought for the paracetamol elixir Rhona had put in her bag, then, after giving some to Song and removing all his clothes except for his nappy, she sponged him down repeatedly with the tepid water supplied by the cabin staff.

His temperature gradually lowered, but suddenly he was sick, thoroughly messing up Rosanna's emerald green crepon jumpsuit, although remaining surprisingly clean himself.

'Have you a change of clothing with you?' asked a sympathetic stewardess.

Trying not to look at Stuart, sure he was disgusted by Song's performance, Rosanna shook her head. 'All my things are in my cases in the hold,' she said disconsolately.

'I think the child was aiming at me and missed,' Stuart surprised her by seeming amused. 'Look, you go and clean yourself up and change into these.' Rummaging in his hand luggage, he drew out a colourful pair of Bermuda shorts and a white T-shirt. 'I bought them in the duty-free shop at the airport,' he explained a little self-consciously. 'I don't know why I did, I just thought they might come in useful some time, although I certainly hadn't an eventuality like this in mind!'

'They'd go round me a dozen times!' Rosanna remonstrated, looking at them.

'Beggars can't be choosers,' Stuart quoted. 'And anything will smell sweeter than the clothes you're wearing. Hurry up, the child's twitching.'

'I can't leave him just now,' Rosanna noticed Song's eyes flick upwards. 'He's gone a bit blue and his breathing's not too good. . .'

'Run along and get changed.' Stuart reverted to his more usual testiness. 'I'll handle him—I'm a doctor too, aren't I? I know what to do when a child's fitting.

See, he's calming down now, he'll be asleep in a minute. Try and get back so that you can hold him. He'd prefer that.'

With which he gave her an appraising up-and-down stare. 'So would anyone with any sense,' he added meaningfully, losing his abrasiveness, Then, wrinkling up his aristocratic nose, 'But *not* when you're in that condition!' he specified.

CHAPTER SIX

GOING back to the small nursery-room, Rosanna had a good wash, thoroughly rinsing out her clothes and putting them into a plastic bag. Finally, wearing the sports garments supplied by Stuart, she studied her reflection in the mirror and winced. The clothes fitted only where they touched!

Feeling—and looking—a bit of a clown, she returned to her seat to find that Song was sleeping peacefully and Stuart himself was dozing. He had Song loosely wrapped in the shawl and was nursing him as if to fatherhood born.

Rosanna stood just looking for a moment, thinking what a pleasant picture they made together. . .the big strong man with features of granite tenderly cuddling a helpless baby, and her heart once again softened towards Stuart.

Unexpectedly he opened his eyes and gently ruffled Song's soft crown of hair.

'We've become good friends,' he said drowsily. 'He even let me put his shirt thing back on. Mind you, I don't think he knew what I was doing, or even who was doing it! How old is he?'

'I don't know exactly,' Rosanna replied unthinkingly. 'Five, possibly six months.'

Stuart nearly exploded. 'What! You don't know the age of your own child? Surely you can remember when he was born?'

Rosanna stayed silent, thinking it best not to answer until she had worked out exactly what it would be safe to say. She could hardly reply that Song was born before she knew anything at all about Rhona or the baby. Being so shrewd, Stuart would soon reason out that Rhona was Song's mother and had taken time off to have him before starting her training in the surgery unit, purposely keeping his imminent birth secret from all hospital staff, even managing to keep news of her pregnancy from Stuart himself when, after interviewing her for the surgeon-in-training job, he had offered her the post and she had accepted it.

Revealing such subterfuge would definitely ruin all her chances of getting a good reference from him, there was no doubt about that. Everyone knew how inflexible his views were.

Rosanna saddened, sorry to be involved in all the deception, sure Stuart would be unable to forgive her for the part she was playing, yet what alternative had she at this late stage?

He would never accept that she had been told little about Song until Rhona was at a loss to know what to do with him because of his aunt being called home to Singapore.

Losing herself in remembering her conversations with Rhona, Rosanna forgot Stuart had asked her a question.

'You're hesitating, seeming very uncertain. . .may I ask why?' He glowered a little. 'At least tell me how you've been keeping all knowledge of the child's existence from everyone. Who's been looking after him, or don't you know that either?' Irony chilled his voice.

'His aunt, down in the village.'

'*His* aunt? Isn't she a relative of yours too?'

Rosanna decided she would have to be extra careful how she dealt with his questions or she might find her replies being held against her in the future, building up a wall of distrust which might prove very hard to break down.

'I'm afraid I'm very confused,' she muttered by way

of excuse. 'Possibly it's the air-conditioning? What do you think?'

'Don't talk nonsense, Rosanna. I know you're hiding something from me. . .being deliberately evasive, for some reason I can't fathom out. Not that I'm particularly interested one way or the other.' He shrugged his wide shoulders as if throwing off the subject, and handing Song over rather abruptly, adjusted his hired headphones and withdrew into the in-flight music world, much to Rosanna's annoyance.

She was needing to get him out of her system and knew an enforced silence would do nothing to help. It simply left her feeling miserable and shut out.

Frustrated, she saw to Song, concentrating on keeping him calm, fearing a growing unrest might trigger off more febrile convulsions.

Nevertheless, in spite of all her efforts to maintain peace the hours dragged and the tensions grew, and Stuart did not help matters by persistently strumming his fingers on the arm of her chair in time to the music only he could hear.

'Oh, do stop!' she burst out eventually, clapping her hand over his to keep it still. 'All this tap-tapping is getting on my nerves!'

'My, my, you prefer holding hands in public?' he gibed, the back of his hand insidiously caressing her palm.

Instantly she pulled her hand away. Sighing, he removed the earphones and reached for the *Straits Times* and *Business Times*, those Singapore newspapers printed in English and supplied free to the business section.

'I was only trying to make friends again,' he commented drily. 'It seems to me that the situation we find ourselves in calls for a robust sense of humour or it will soon become intolerable. What mood are you in now?' He reached for a paper again.

'A bad one. I can't see a thing when you open those pages out so wide!' Rosanna complained, still feeling at odds with the world and inclined to blame Stuart, although she wasn't sure why.

He glanced at her strained face. 'I think you're in need of a siesta,' he said, folding the newspapers away. 'Let's take turns at sleeping on each other's shoulder. You managed very well once, I remember.'

Rosanna blushed in spite of her resolve not to.

'Come alone, move over and cuddle up,' Stuart invited. 'Take your chance while the child's quiet.' He looked over at Song solicitously. 'He seems poorly, is he all right?'

'Of course he is,' Rosanna returned with an enforced air of confidence, desperately trying to hide the disquiet aroused by Stuart's words. From experience she knew that 'poorly' in his surgical vocabulary had an ominous ring to it.

Noting Song's increasing pallor, she raised concerned eyes to Stuart.

'He needs proper medical attention,' he said. 'Something we can't possibly give him here. There aren't the facilities.'

'I know, and I'm growing scared,' Rosanna confessed. 'I'll be jolly glad when I can hand him over to Tang. He's a prominent doctor in the New Singapore General Hospital, so he should be able to get him the immediate attention he needs.'

'Is Tang the name of the boy's father?' Stuart asked unceremoniously, shooting the question at her as if to leave no time for a devious answer to be thought up.

Wearying of having to avoid the truth, Rosanna nodded, 'Yes, if you must know.'

'But you said you weren't married?'

Although now in the mood to explain and have the whole matter cleared up, for Rhona's sake Rosanna decided not to commit herself one way or the other.

Instead she moved over to a seat by another window and peered out. 'Oh, look!' she called to Stuart, her ruffled feelings discounted in the excitement of the moment. 'There's a strange world of sampans and skyscrapers approaching!'

Stuart took the seat beside her, leaned over and fastened both her seatbelt and Song's infant version. 'We're coming in to land,' he said, just as the tannoy voice confirmed it, warning everyone to fasten seatbelts.

Leaning quite unnecessarily close, or so it seemed to Rosanna, he made the excuse of having to adjust the belts, saying he had left them too loose. Immediately her heart reacted in the strangest way to his touch, beating irregularly, leaping around, leaving her breathless.

'What's the matter?' he asked, noticing her surreptitiously checking her pulse.

'Nothing,' she said. 'My heart started misbehaving a little—a touch of indigestion, that's all it was.'

'Indigestion? That's an insult to the airline! The meals served on the flight have been superb. No, whatever's wrong with you, it can't be indigestion.' He studied her thoughtfully. 'But you have lost your colour for some reason or other.' He put a hand on her wrist. 'Your heart's racing like mad! Is this what my nearness does to you, Rosanna?'

Immediately colour simply flooded her cheeks and she drew back, but the sudden humour softening the lines of his face was hard to resist. It called for a lighthearted response from her, so, forgetting all her worries concerning him, she actually smiled back.

'That's better.' Tipping her face up towards his, he looked deep into her eyes. 'I find you very attractive, you know. Can't you try to like me just a little?'

Aware of the feelings he was arousing, Rosanna trembled but remained silent.

'Your belt needs adjusting again.' With a surprisingly mischievous air Stuart put his arm around her and quite unnecessarily took hold of the belt. With feelings much too disturbed for comfort by this time, she clasped Song to her for protection.

Stuart half-laughed. 'You don't trust me, do you, but I'm really not such an ogre as you think!' His lopsided smile made one of its rare appearances, turning her heart over. She scarcely knew what to do with herself.

'Watch it,' Stuart warned teasingly, 'or before you know it you'll be falling in love!'

Which was exactly what she was frightened of, not that she knew what it was like to be in love, but— conscious of his breath warm on her cheeks, his face so near, lips so temptingly close, all combining to create havoc inside her—she was left in little doubt as to what ailed her.

The unimaginable had happened. . .and with Stuart Gainsborough of all people! Rosanna chided herself for being so susceptible, but she knew it was too late for her to halt the surge of romantic feelings building up and threatening to overwhelm her.

She found she could hardly take her eyes off Stuart, no longer seeing only an irascible surgeon who invariably introduced a sour note into hospital life, but taking note instead of the caring, honest eyes, the lines of ready humour, and the lips that were no longer grim and tightened into a thin line, but soft and so inviting that hers parted involuntarily, waiting for, longing for, his kiss.

But nothing happened. Stuart and Rosanna simply remained gazing at each other as if sharing a vision of a glorious and magical wonderworld.

The plane came in to land quite unnoticed by either of them. Only on the final bump did Stuart stir and turn his attention to Song.

'You'll need to use both arms to carry him,' he murmured, his voice surprisingly gentle and understanding, almost as if he were conscious of the ring of enchantment still enfolding Rosanna and not wishing to break it.

'He'll tire you out,' he insisted, releasing the seatbelts.

Carrying her hand luggage with his own, he led the way from plane to travalator, then on the escalator to the arrival hall on the recently added storey of the six-storey terminal.

Although Song was still struggling, tiring Rosanna's efforts to hold him, there was a dreamy quality about her movements, so, looking quizzically at her and realising she was still in something of a reverie, Stuart took her passport out of her bag to show it for her, together with the immigration card all passengers had to fill in when on the plane.

'You'll get the stub back. Keep it with your passport, then surrender it on departure from the Republic,' he reminded her thoughtfully.

The mention of a passport brought Rosanna speedily back down to earth. She watched, wide-eyed and fearful, as he flipped through the empty pages of hers.

'There's nothing here about the boy,' he exclaimed, puzzling over them just as she had feared he might.

'No, but it doesn't matter, he has his own passport. There wasn't time to get things properly organised. I'll get it,' she muddled through her explanation, hoping he wouldn't ask any more questions, and freeing one hand—almost dropping Song in the process—she reached out to take her bag from Stuart, not wanting him to see the name Song had been registered under.

For it was Rhona's maiden name. Like many female doctors she still used the name she had qualified under, and had thought it best to keep Song's surname the same as hers until he and she moved to Singapore and permanently adopted Tang's name.

Stuart, being so shrewd, would soon put two and two together were he to see the passport, Rosanna reminded herself fearfully, sure that then all the new-found harmony would disappear in a flurry of anger and disillusionment, something she wanted to avoid at all costs.

So, in near panic, she dodged Stuart as she had in the departure lounge before the flight, managing to show the passport herself before he knew where she was. Then she escaped into the arrival hall where Tang and his sister were already waiting.

As had been arranged beforehand, they had booked one of the day-rooms and were watching for her to join them, Tang standing just inside the doorway.

There was no need for Nimi to introduce him, as Rosanna had met him before when he had helped Rhona move in with her, although she had not known at the time that he was Rhona's husband, only that he was a friend over on a short holiday from Singapore. Now, of course, she knew he had flown over to England to be present at his son's birth.

His face lit up with joy at the sight of Song, and coming forward, he took him in his arms. Watching out for Stuart, Rosanna gave him a quick account of the worrying episode of febrile convulsions.

Immediately, concern for the child overriding all other matters, Tang and Nimi whisked him away to the hospital. Feeling free to be herself again, a load off her mind, Rosanna went in search of Stuart. She soon found him.

'Where have you been? And where's the boy?' he enquired at once.

'I told you, I had to hand him over to his father,' she answered defensively, fearing he was about to take her to task once again, and spoil everything just when she thought she had saved the situation.

'It didn't take you long. Where was he?' Stuart frowned, none too pleased. 'I'd like to have spoken to him about the child's condition. Couldn't you have introduced us?'

'There was no time for niceties. He was very worried about the boy and hurried him along to the hospital immediately.'

'Didn't you want to go with him?'

'It wasn't necessary, and I couldn't really leave you stranded without knowing what was happening, could I? Look, I've *got* to get into some decent clothes. Where's our hotel?'

'You're a cool customer,' Stuart shook an admonishing head over her. 'Haven't you any maternal instincts at all?'

'Few when I'm dressed like this,' Rosanna retorted. 'I don't know what the family must have thought of me.'

'Are you seeing them again?'

'Oh, of course.'

'Then make sure you're dressed up to the nines next time and they'll forget what you were wearing today. I'll come and help you choose something appropriate. I've been reading particulars about this airport while I've been wandering around looking for you. There's a total of forty-seven shops within this passenger terminal, imagine that! Come along to the viewing mall on the third storey and choose one you fancy.'

'*I* know quite a bit about Changi airport too,' Rosanna said, perking up. 'The second terminal has only just been opened and a skytrain runs between the two terminals, giving passengers a choice of over ninety-six shops, not just forty-seven. Whatever you read must have been out of date! And did you realise that when shopping at the mezzanine level one can see the departure activities of the lower level? See, I know this mini-city of an airport better than you think.'

'Where did *you* get your information?' Stuart looked interested.

'From. . .' Rosanna stopped, horrified. She had been about to say Rhona! 'Oh, does it matter? Let's go to the viewing mall and do some shopping.' She looked down at herself and grimaced. 'I'll see what the shops can provide! Anyway, in this heat I'm going to want cooler things than I've brought with me. If it's as hot as this in an air-conditioned place, imagine what it must be like outside!'

'At just one degree north of the Equator I suppose one can expect it to be hot with light showers for nine months of the year, hot with occasional monsoon downpours for three. . .in other words, it never varies from hot and sultry, is monotonously predictable, the temperature never varying by more than two degrees Celsius, averaging twenty-seven degrees day to day.'

'So you've read the notice I've read!' Rosanna didn't wait to hear more. She hurried to a fashion shop, to return a very short time later in a flower-patterned wraparound polycotton pareo worn—as instructed by the shop assistant—leaving both arms bare, but with some of the material draped gracefully around one side of the neck, a flimsy matching scarf worn around the waist as a belt.

Stuart eyed her in surprise. 'It suits you,' he acceded, a gleam of admiration in his eyes. 'Suits you much better than your more usual grimy white coat!'

'Even better than a man's Bermuda shorts and T-shirt?' Rosanna asked impishly, beginning to feel cheerful again, especially as she felt justified in optimistically believing she had resolved the problem of Song without giving anything away which could possibly ruin Rhona's prospects.

Stuart nodded, his expression well controlled.

'The girl in the shop called it a cocktail pareo, but I suppose it could be worn anywhere, for any occasion?' Rosanna twirled rather self-consciously, then, in more diffident vein, waited to hear his opinion.

'Um, yes, it looks fine,' Stuart obliged, adding with a calculating look, 'Do you think your husband will like it?'

Rosanna sighed. 'Surely I told you? I haven't got a husband.'

Stuart's eyes dulled. 'I'm beginning to disbelieve everything you say,' he spoke chastisingly. 'You're surprising me at every turn. What about speaking the truth for a change, Rosanna? Exactly what sort of a girl are you under that deceivingly cool exterior?'

'I don't know what you mean.' Trying desperately hard, Rosanna hid her rising distress.

'I'm referring to the fact that Peter Armstrong had lipstick on his face after you said goodbye to him, and no doubt the mysterious Tang has just enjoyed the same privilege. . .so tell me, is this added allure of yours——' he gave the pareo a significant glance '—meant to impress me? Are you aiming to add *me* to your list. Because if so. . .'

'That was an uncalled-for remark!' Rosanna interrupted, her eyes narrowing angrily. 'Could it be that you're jealous, Mr Gainsborough?' She curled up inside, waiting for a hurtful rejoinder.

But a deprecating 'Huh!' was all the reply Stuart gave before turning away to hail a taxi to take them to their luxury hotel.

However, he had the grace to say, 'I'm sorry,' when in the lift speeding them up to the tenth floor after they passed through hotel reception, and reaching for Rosanna's hand, he pressed it between both of his. 'Don't let's mess up this once-in-a-lifetime holiday by quarrelling. Am I forgiven?' he asked.

As she looked up at him, Rosanna's wrath died an

instant death and she knew she could be tempted to forgive him almost anything.

He slipped an arm about her shoulders and peering down at her, smiled disarmingly. She coloured, weakening under his touch, and inadvertently leaned closer—before remembering the need to distance herself from him, physically as well as mentally, in order to continue protecting Rhona's secret.

So she shrugged him off. It seemed the only thing to do under the circumstances, but of course Stuart misunderstood. Dropping his arm, he moved away, scowling a little, obviously displeased.

'What do the others have that I haven't?' he muttered vexedly, but the lift stopped at that moment, saving Rosanna from having to think up an acceptable reply.

'Adjoining rooms?' Stuart raised his eyebrows, unlocking one door after surveying the luxuriously furnished landing with its numbered doors. 'Two *single* rooms were reserved for us by the looks of it, so what will happen if your husband wants to stay with you, the baby too?'

'He won't—they won't—oh, you're confusing me!' Rosanna stood up to him. 'I told you, I haven't got a husband. As for little Song, he's far better off in hospital having the treatment he needs.'

'You refer to him in a very strange way,' said Stuart. 'That's what I can't understand about you. There's something odd about all this. In our hospital you're known as a caring doctor, yet you appear to be singularly detached from your own child. It just doesn't add up!'

He opened one of the bedroom doors and prepared to open the other.

'You worry at me like a dog at a bone,' Rosanna complained, sighing wearily.

'Well, reassure me. Show some natural feelings

towards the boy.' Stuart dumped her cases inside the room and handed her the door keys. 'Sure enough, you did all you could for him on the way over, but with such an impersonal, "only doing one's duty" attitude.'

Rosanna made no attempt to answer.

'I see there's a connecting door between our rooms,' he continued. 'We'll keep it locked, shall we?' Then he went into his own room, a pageboy having already placed his luggage in there for him.

Rosanna closed the door and turned the key in the connecting door. Then, and only then, did she give way to tears.

Rhona, she was thinking, couldn't have known the problems she was giving her. . .or the heartache and unhappiness the problems were bringing with them.

But then Rhona was unaware of the attraction she was feeling towards Stuart. . .an attraction which she was having to keep at bay, even try to deny. Holidaying with him in such an exotic place as Singapore could have been so wonderful; instead she was having to spoil everything for him, as well as for herself.

The flow of tears increased.

A knock came on the connecting door, and opening it, she found herself face to face with Stuart again.

'Crying?' He reached out a hand to wipe a tear away. 'So you do have feelings?' There was an unexpected tenderness in his voice. 'Well, don't cry any more, freshen yourself up and we'll go out and have a look around this amazing island. And Rosanna, if I caused any of those tears, I'm sorry.' Then leaning forward, he kissed her lightly on both cheeks.

'They're salty!' He licked his lips with such a surprised expression on his face that Rosanna couldn't suppress a chuckle, which inadvertently turned into hiccups, setting both Stuart and herself off laughing again, all dissension melting away once more.

'Drink some cold water from the wrong side of the

cup,' Stuart suggested, sobering down. 'I'm told the drinking water is perfectly safe to drink here. I won't stay and watch your performance or I might start hiccupping myself! I give you just about half an hour to be ready to leave the hotel with me, and we'll visit the hospital first and foremost—how's that?'

Rosanna made her hiccups an excuse not to answer. Stuart was trying to be understanding, she realised that, but oh, how she wished she need not visit Song in his company! For all she knew Tang and his relatives might be there too and she would have another battle on her hands to keep Stuart from finding out Rhona's secret!

All the same, come what may, she needed to be with Stuart. The yearning she was experiencing for the first time was too hard to resist. Every second in his company was becoming precious to her, especially as she felt the time would soon come when he would be rightfully disillusioned and not wish to have anything further to do with her.

Gingerly touching her cheeks, remembering the feel and the thrill of his lips as they rested on them for that brief second, she caught her breath in wonder, ecstasy almost within reach.

Only Stuart would be able to bring it closer. She would need him to share it with her. It would be a glorious feeling. . .glorious beyond anything she had ever known. A gossamer rainbow of happiness would float around her like a cloak when he took her in his arms. . .it would be an exquisite moment. . .

She closed her eyes, wistfully daydreaming, then a tear escaped from under her eyelids and ran down beside her short nose, tickling it and bringing her back to reality. There would be no rapture, no happiness. She had lost the chance of it by cheating Stuart.

He would never forgive her for deceiving him and

putting Rhona's needs before his own. Woefully she dried her tears.

Then, her natural optimism coming to the fore, she decided to make the most of the two weeks she would have with him and not allow herself to look ahead to the blank days she would have to live through when he found out the truth about her.

She was ready for him well before the allotted time was up, brightening herself up by wearing the only evening dress she had brought with her, a turquoise velvet-look off-the-shoulder-gown which undoubtedly showed her figure off to perfection and put a glow over her fair skin.

Then suddenly the rumour Rhona had repeated came back to strike a bitter cold chord in her heart.

According to the hospital grapevine, Stuart was a married man!

CHAPTER SEVEN

'WE'VE struck lucky!' Coming into her room half an hour or so later, Stuart greeted Rosanna with a gratified smile. 'We're here in time for the Mooncake Festival!'

She took a final peep at herself in the beautifully scroll-edged wall-mirror, wanting to make sure no telltale signs of recent tears remained.

'Mooncake Festival?' she echoed. 'What's that?'

'Only one of the most important occasions on the lunar calendar. But of course *you* would know it better by its Singaporean title. . . *Zhong Qiu Jie*?' His smile was lopsided and taunting, the cleft in his strong chin more noticeably attractive than ever.

He's amusing himself at my expense, thought Rosanna, wishing she could reply in as light a vein but unable to do so because she was still having to act in such an underhand way, having realised that at all costs she must keep Stuart away from Song while Tang and Nimi were with him.

'It won't be necessary for us to visit the hospital,' she blurted out. 'Tang's just been on the phone, and everything's fine.'

'Oh,' said Stuart, and that was all. But after a short pause, 'It's no good, Rosanna,' he shook his head reprovingly, 'I know there hasn't been a phone call, just as I know that for some reason or other you don't want me to meet this Tang you mention.'

Rosanna stood, eyes downcast, not knowing what to say.

'You're hopeless at pretending—admit it, now,' he continued banteringly.

He won't think I'm so hopeless at pretending when he knows how I've been misleading him about Song, she thought miserably, misgivings crowding in on her again.

'Well, I won't probe; all I want is to enjoy this free holiday.' Stuart took a brightly coloured pamphlet from his pocket. 'This tells us all about mooncakes, and very interesting it is too—even gives recipes. Mooncakes are shaped round, representing the full moon at harvest time. Just about as many legends surround them as the variety of fillings put into them.'

'All the same, I don't want to try *any* sort of cake, if you don't mind,' Rosanna muttered, glad nevertheless of the change of subject. 'I'd rather save my appetite for the evening dinner arranged for us.'

'Same here,' Stuart agreed. 'I wasn't really wanting to leave the hotel before the meal, I simply presumed *you* might be in a hurry to visit the hospital. However,' he shrugged his shoulders uncaringly, 'if you're satisfied the boy's all right, that's fine by me. We'll try mooncakes another time, but if you feel up to it later on this evening we'll take a sightseeing trip just to get the feel of our surroundings. . .how about that?'

'Would I have to change into other clothes?' Rosanna was suddenly determined to have him notice the flattering off-the-shoulder, bouffant-skirted gown she was wearing.

He appraised her from head to toe with no change of expression. 'Not for my sake,' he said, 'but then you're not out to please me, are you, so just suit yourself.' Nonchalantly he dismissed the matter without another glance in her direction, much to her chagrin.

'There's a spectacular blaze of colour in Chinatown's shops, streets and houses in the evenings, lanterns of all shapes and sizes hanging out everywhere, reds and golds predominating,' he read on from the leaflet he was still holding, adding with a debating glance, his eyebrows lifting, 'They might be worth viewing?'

'Sounds like it.' Rosanna spoke without enthusiasm, however. She was far from sure she had the energy to go out anywhere, no matter what the temptation. The evening she had begun to look forward to suddenly seemed to lack lustre, draining her of all vitality. What had been the point of dressing up to impress? she asked herself. Stuart was obviously not at all interested in her, nor in what she wore. She could have been covered in sackcloth for all he had deigned to notice. Just think of those ghastly shorts and the T-shirt he had given her to wear!

She drew a deep breath, aghast at herself for her lack of gratitude. What was the matter with her? she wondered. Could it be that she was aiming to attract him? Surely not.

No, all she wanted was to be on good terms with him for two weeks. After that they could return to their old stand against each other. It was no business of hers whether or not he had a wife and children, although naturally she would be sympathetic if he chose to pour out his troubles to her. If he didn't she would not feel thwarted in any way. Of course not.

But suddenly, almost as if sensing her uneasy state of mind, Stuart tucked her arm companionably through his and walked her out to the glittering glass-walled lift, then, after descending in it to the ground floor, took her along towards the hotel's premier restaurant.

'I had a quick browse through the information booklets left in my room,' he told her, putting his arm round her shoulder in a friendly way. 'I expect there was a similar supply in yours. . .did you vet them?'

'I was too busy doing other things,' Rosanna sighed. 'Like crying over you', she could have added had she wished him to know how he affected her, but the last thing she wanted was for him to realise the havoc he was creating in her heart.

Not that she considered it portended anything serious, it was merely the result of extreme exhaustion, or so she assured herself, resolutely denying any possiblity that he could have had a disrupting effect on her emotions.

Nevertheless, in spite of deliberately tossing aside all thoughts of romance, she remained remarkably conscious of the warmth of his arm and had to be very stern with herself not to nestle back into it.

He looked down at her, his hand touching her bare shoulder, and although for no longer than it took to draw breath his fingers lingered on her skin, it was long enough for her to experience a strange thrill and feelings such as she had never even dreamed existed.

Remaining sensitive to the gentle caress even after she and Stuart had moved slighly apart, she wondered whether it had been intended or accidental. There was no way of knowing.

She looked up at him questioningly and in that instant lost all sense of reality, her world seeming to turn dizzily topsy-turvy. Had it not been for Stuart's quick reaction, she would have fallen to the floor, losing her balance because everything seemed to be spinning around her.

Instantly clasping her to him, however, he managed to keep her on her feet, but only by holding her so close that they might well have been bonded together.

Nothing was said for a moment, then, he said wryly, his voice slightly husky, 'My diagnosis is that food is what's needed in your case. For me? A new much tougher heart. I'm sure you send my ECG skyrocketing! I confess I'm at a loss to know what to do about you.'

Her own moment of rapture having taken her by storm, Rosanna suddenly fully realised the danger she was in, warning herself uneasily that if she didn't watch out she would fall hopelessly, incredibly in love—and with Stuart, of all people! Stuart, a man with a failed marriage notched up against him.

The sadness in the thought was almost more than she could bear, so it came as a relief to have the *maître d'hôtel* suddenly come up to announce that their table had been prepared. He escorted them to it.

'What a time for him to intrude! I'd forgotten the world still existed!' Stuart muttered as he sat down. 'I'm in a very romantic mood, Rosanna. . .but oh, I'm forgetting—you're married, aren't you?'

'*I'm* not, but you are!' she blurted out, distressed.

He froze. 'What do you mean?' he asked angrily.

'You accuse me of being secretive, but what about you?'

'What about me?' Stuart challenged, his voice hardening.

'Oh, nothing, just let's eat.' In a subdued voice Rosanna added, 'What are you going to choose?'

'I'm choosing to be happy, at least for the length of the holiday,' he replied curtly. 'Anything wrong with that?'

'I meant. . .what are you going to choose for starters?' Rosanna, hiding her hurt feelings, stared pointedly at the menu card.

Studying her face, Stuart softened. 'I knew what you meant,' he admitted with a surprising gentleness.

Capitulating to his changed mood, she struggled to quieten the qualms of guilt troubling her on account of the trick she and Rhona were playing on him.

And, needing to feel better about deceiving him, she reminded herself—for the umpteenth time—that Rhona was a good doctor who deserved help.

So what right had Stuart to allow his prejudices against working doctor-mothers to ruin Rhona's life? No right at all, she argued. . .hoping to persuade herself she was perfectly justified in doing what she was doing.

Yet doubts kept creeping in, so, to help herself along, she kept her eyes averted from him in case the magnetism he seemed able to exert at will unsettled her again.

'You're wrapped up in your own thoughts once more,' he protested. 'Couldn't you spare me just a little of your attention?'

There was no time for her to reply before they were being served in the sumptuously decorated room. Golden candelabra on every table reflected the soft sparkling light from the diamond glass chandeliers above. Exquisitely sculptured decorative candles complemented beautiful flower arrangements.

'I only hope the food will be as good as its magnificent setting,' mused Stuart, looking around.

He had no need to worry. Thinly sliced air-dried beef and Parma ham with cornichons, followed by chilled courgette soup served with gnocchi of pink pimento led on to the main course—poached *ikan kurau* served with Keta caviare in watercress sauce. Everything had been cooked superbly well and proved absolutely delicious.

After an ample serving of tropical fruit cocktail with homemade fruit sherbet, helped along by another half-glass of the excellent champagne Mr Armstrong Senior had ordered to be served to Stuart and herself with each luncheon or dinner, Rosanna declared she wanted nothing more than a good sleep.

'You can sleep tonight,' Stuart replied, showing no sympathy even when, with eyes drowsily half-closed and elbows resting on the edge of the table, she needed to support her chin with her fists in order to prevent her head from drooping.

'Mind the flowers!' He moved the bowl of multi-coloured orchids aside on the delicately crocheted lace tablecloth. 'Orchids are Singapore's national flower,' he told her while examining one of the rare blooms. 'They thrive in the humid heat. . .or didn't you know that either?' he smiled teasingly.

Rosanna tried to blink herself more awake. 'At this moment I don't know anything. Oh, dear, I'm sorry I'm slurring my words. . . I think I must be suffering from jet-lag.'

'Oh, come on, you can suffer from that later on if you want to, but not right now. Rouse yourself!' Stuart pushed her coffee cup towards her. 'I want to go out and see the sights, and I want to see them with you.'

Reminded of Peter Armstrong's self-same words but feeling differently about them because this time it was Stuart speaking, Rosanna roused herself sufficiently to sip some coffee and stand up.

Then, as on a sudden thought, she declared she was just going to slip up to her room for a light scarf, and before Stuart could stop her she walked as briskly as she could away from the table and out to the lifts, not wanting to give him time to follow her in case he had already guessed she had something more on her mind than fetching a scarf—for he could scarcely have failed to notice that the tropical evening was far too warm for the need of any extra covering.

He was waiting by the lift when she came down in it. He frowned. 'I see no scarf,' he charged, after a shrewd up-and-down glance over her neat figure.

'Oh, I—I forgot it!' She coloured guiltily.

'You phoned the hospital, didn't you?' he accused mildly. 'That was what you went up for, not for a scarf at all. But why didn't you want me to know? Surely you realise I'd have been disappointed in you if you hadn't taken the opportunity to enquire about your child? It worried me when you let the little fellow go out of your care so readily. Quite extraordinary—very unnatural.' Then his voice softened again. 'By the way, how is he?'

'Asleep and in a stable condition.' She made no effort to contradict his assumption that she had intended phoning the hospital when she went up to her room. There seemed little purpose in adding to her deceit where he was concerned.

'So that's OK.' He perked up. 'No point in us visiting him at the moment, we might disturb him. After the trouble he had on the long flight he'll need all the sleep he can get. Which leaves us free to go out and paint the town red, so come on!'

Obviously determining to throw all cares to the wind, he strode forward to stand tall and eager between the majestic portals of the hotel entrance. Certainly he looked impressive, Rosanna thought, siding with the opinion Rhona had expressed. Not handsome necessarily, but impressive. Obedient to the command in his voice, she moved towards him.

'What a feast of vibrant shades!' he exclaimed, looking out towards the bustling streets, reflections from the hundreds of multi-coloured lanterns dancing in the blue of his deep-set eyes.

He hailed a passing trishaw. 'These are new to us,' he said. 'And new experiences are half the fun of a holiday, don't you agree?' Helping Rosanna into the sidecar, he sat on the seat beside her.

'It seems rough on the cyclist, having two adult passengers to pull along.' She glanced sympathetically towards the Singaporean riding on the bike connected to the sidecar.

'Well used to it, I expect.' Stuart sat back, relaxing. 'His way of making a living. Anyway, it's not as if we're going uphill. But look around you, Rosanna— have you ever seen a sight like this before?'

'Never! A whole kaleidoscope of colours! And such bustling crowds too, people of every nationality herding peacefully together. . .lovely!' She felt her tiredness slipping away in her eagerness to see all there was to see.

'A world of many cultures.' Stuart reached forward to get hold of her hand. 'Let's get out and walk, we'll get the feel of the place better that way.'

Dismissing the trishaw rider, but overpaying him generously, he led the way down Chinatown to the waterfront, exploring a maze of streets and peering in numerous old shophouses on the way, seeing craftsmen still at work making theatre masks, lion heads, carving in all mediums, and even making paper replicas of houses, cars, and all sorts of modern luxury goods.

'Why take all that trouble only to set fire to the things?' Rosanna asked after hearing that the paper models would be burnt at funerals.

'Well, from what I've read,' Stuart told her, 'some folk still believe that they can ease the deceased person's way to Paradise by providing them with worldly goods represented by the paper houses, cars and luxury articles, even putting specially printed million-dollar Singaporean notes into the coffins. Not that they're legal tender in this world, of course, otherwise we'd be millionaires this minute, as identical notes have been left with the leaflets in our rooms.'

'Oh, look!' Rosanna stopped outside a building called Meow Choon Foh Yit Kee. 'What do you think this place is?'

Stuart consulted one of the leaflets he still carried in his pocket. 'It should be of interest to us,' he said. 'It's a traditional Chinese medical hall. The pharmacist selects centuries-old remedies from dozens of drawers inscribed with Chinese characters. Powder scratched from an antelope's horn, for instance, supposedly relieves high fevers.'

'Let's take some back to our hospital with us, then,'

Rosanna suggested facetiously. 'Intensive Care could do with some help.'

'You're tired—either that or you've developed a jaded sense of humour!' Stuart half-laughed. 'Well, let's go back to the hotel. We'll make an early start tomorrow. I'm keen to see some of the parks, the zoo, and the Crocodilarium where over a thousand crocodiles are fed at certain times and wrestle every day except Mondays and rainy days.'

He actually chuckled at the face she pulled. 'Or if you prefer it,' he continued, producing another leaflet, 'we could watch hundreds of alligators, snakes and lizards being fed between eleven a.m. and three. They're bred for their skins, apparently.'

'Ugh!' Rosanna shivered. 'Put away those horrid papers! I don't want to watch the poor creatures, knowing the fate that awaits them!'

'Then perhaps you'd rather attend a bird-singing concert?'

'Have you a notice about that too? Are the birds going to be killed after they've sung?'

'No, the Singaporeans love birds as much as we do. Proud owners bring them in beautiful cages which are then hung up outside a coffee shop each Sunday morning. I don't know which coffee shop, but we'll find out tomorrow. That's if you'd like to go there?'

'Very much so, especially if you let me catch up on some sleep tonight.'

'It's a bargain,' said Stuart, beginning to yawn himself. Hailing a taxi, he took her back to the hotel. Outside her room they stopped, each of them seeming reluctant to part. They stood together, not touching, not even looking at one another.

Finally Stuart broke the silence. 'Do I get a goodnight kiss?' he asked with a surprisingly winsome charm. 'I don't think I'll manage to get to sleep without one.'

Rosanna laughed a little self-consciously, stood up on tiptoe, raised her face to his expectantly, then suddenly dropped back on her heels, straining away from him.

'I don't flirt with married men,' she declared stalwartly, although quite unable to hide the sob in her voice.

'A very laudable principle,' Stuart agreed, reaching out and kissing her just the same.

'Oh!' She tried to sound indignant, and breaking away she fumbled with the key in her lock, her hands trembling.

'Here, let me.' He took over from her and had the door open in a flash. 'Goodnight, now,' he said, a challenge in his voice, a barely hidden invitation in his deep-set eyes.

Pushing past him, Rosanna entered her room and quickly shut the door behind her before leaning back against it, breathing deeply in an attempt to quieten down her agitated heart.

CHAPTER EIGHT

WHEN Stuart knocked on Rosanna's door to go with her down to breakfast the following morning there was no reply. After waiting for some minutes, knocking repeatedly, he gave up, went down to reception and asked if anyone knew where she was.

But before there was time for an answer, she walked in through the opulent entrance.

'You've been to the hospital?' he greeted her, seeming sure his guess was right when she coloured with embarrassment. 'Do you think it wise for you to travel about on your own in a strange country—or isn't it so very strange to you?' he continued challengingly.

Rosanna glared back at him, wondering what he was getting at and thinking he sounded more like a sceptical schoolteacher than a man who had thrilled her so much the previous evening.

'I took a taxi both ways,' she answered, very much on her dignity.

'So I should hope!' He remained tetchy.

Her mouth firmed. 'I'm quite capable of looking after myself, you know. I've been doing it for long enough!'

'And succeeding more by luck than good judgement, I'll be bound!'

Her grey eyes hardened, the green flecks becoming steely.

'I don't know what's going on,' Stuart growled, 'but obviously I'm not meant to know. Is it something you're ashamed of? Is that it?'

His assumption was so near the mark that Rosanna's cheeks blazed guiltily, but after puzzling over her for a

92

moment or two Stuart suddenly softened his approach, put a hand on her shoulder and said, 'It's all right. You don't have to tell me if you don't want to,' then, with the semblance of an understanding smile, he went on to suggest that it was about time they went in to have breakfast.

Rosanna felt lost. She could make neither head nor tail of Stuart, she decided, nevertheless, hunger forcing her along, she accompanied him to the dining-room.

'I should have asked you about the boy's health instead of going off the deep end about you slipping away on your own,' Stuart said between the fruit-accompanied cereal and the next course. 'How is he?'

'Fine.'

'I can't help being curious. There's some mystery attached to him, isn't there?'

Anxious to keep him in a good mood, Rosanna decided to tell him as much as she could without involving Rhona, instead using a mythical girl to illustrate her story.

'You mean to say the boy's existence has to be kept secret because otherwise his mother would lose the chance of promotion?' Stuart was openly scandalised.

'Some men are very chauvinistic in that respect,' Rosanna pointed out, greatly daring, careful not to look up at him in case he saw the accusation in her eyes.

'Um, yes,' Stuart half agreed. 'All the same. . .' he paused as if inwardly debating the issue.

'You were saying. . .?' she prompted.

'Oh, hang it all, Rosanna, I know you've heard me express views you might consider chauvinistic, but I wouldn't penalise a mother just because she's a mother. There'd have to be some other fundamental reason why she wasn't suited to her job—sheer incompetence, lack of crucial knowledge, acute laziness, lack of interest. . .that sort of thing. By the way, what *does* the boy's mother do?'

'Here comes our next course.' Rosanna purposely distracted him, then, as she sat back to be served, she decided to counter his question with one of her own.

'Where are your daughters now?' she asked.

Stuart stared at her as if she had gone mad. 'My *what*?' he spluttered.

'Oh, I'm sorry if I've touched you on a raw spot,' Rosanna was genuinely apologetic. 'Only I heard that you'd been left alone with two daughters to care for.'

'Two, have I? Well, that's news to me.' His knife clattered to his plate. 'And from where did you gather that extraordinary information? The hospital grapevine?'

Now I've put my foot in it again, Rosanna thought, seeing his angry frown reappearing, so she decided to speak frankly and get the dissension over as quickly as possible.

'I believe it came from there.' She kept her head lowered. 'Why, isn't it true about your wife deserting you and the girls?'

Stuart seemed unable to speak for a moment or two, almost as if something blocked his throat, but eventually, appearing to gulp the words rather than speak them, he said, his shoulders shaking, 'It just shows that people will believe anything if they want to enough.'

Rosanna watched with a fixed stare, trying to figure whether he was amused or upset by her query.

'Gossip is always lapped up hungrily, no one bothering to check whether or not it has any foundation,' he continued when he could. 'I suppose I should be annoyed, but there's also a comical side to all this.' He laughed outright as if enjoying the joke. 'Oh, Rosanna, don't look so troubled! Does it really matter so much to you whether or not I'm married?'

Knowing how much it did matter, she was unable to

reply. Instead, she waited, not finding the situation at all funny. Was Stuart about to deny the break-up of his marriage? she wondered, then closed her eyes in an attempt to blot out the memory of the kiss which had left her so vulnerable. A kiss he had stolen in spite of her vehement assertion that she didn't flirt with married men.

Surely he didn't think her easy prey? Talk about being a chauvinist! Surely he was the world's worst! He had shown no regard for her feelings, not for those of his wife. No wonder she had deserted him!. . . If she had?

He pushed his plate aside, the cooked breakfast almost untouched. Then his hand reached across the table to clasp hers.

'I am *not* married, Rosanna, have *never* been married.' His eyes looked directly into hers with such apparent candour that she knew he was speaking the truth, and in spite of the aggravation he had caused a few moments before, she felt the beginnings of a wonderful hope rising in her heart.

Still she was lost for words. All she could do was wait to hear what else he had to say.

'The grapevine must have mistaken me for my brother. He too is a doctor, and he's the one with marital problems. When his wife left him he had a breakdown and had to go away for treatment—meanwhile I took over the care of his two young daughters, my nieces. They're now boarders in the convent high school where they used to be day scholars.'

'You don't have to tell me all this,' Rosanna muttered. 'I'm sorry if I made things awkward for you by repeating the grapevine rumour. I should have known better.'

'I'm telling you because it means a lot to me to have you know the truth.' Stuart's hand-clasp strengthened. 'I don't particularly care about what others believe.

Those who matter already know the true facts.' He pressed her hand. 'Especially now,' he added meaningfully.

'How *is* your brother?' asked Rosanna, her eyes downcast because she still felt ashamed of her previous outburst.

'Well enough under the circumstances. Do you want to have anything more to eat, or shall we go out now?' Stuart seemed anxious to have his thoughts diverted from his brother's unhappiness. Either that, thought Rosanna, or there was something else worrying him.

She was soon to find out what it was.

Hiring a taxi, he gave the driver directions to take them to the General Hospital. As she overheard, Rosanna's spirits sank again. Was Stuart determined to solve what to him was the mystery surrounding Song? Perhaps he hadn't believed her any more than she had previously believed him? Was he aiming to confront Tang?

But no. Seemingly his main interest lay in finding out more about the history of medicine in Singapore.

'The first hospital here was a mere shed put up for the care of troops.' Rosanna hoped that if she gave him some information she had gathered from Rhona he would be content not to actually go to the hospital himself. 'There've been five generations of hospitals since,' she added. 'This new one, built in 1975, was restructured in 1989 and has seventeen hundred beds.'

'You know a lot about it, don't you?' Stuart eyed her quizzically as they drove along. 'But did you also know that Singapore was named Temasek or "Sea Town" until the thirteenth century. . .'

'When the Prince of Palembang landed, saw what he thought was a lion with a red body and black head, and renamed the island from two Sanskrit words, *Singa* or lion, and *Pura* or city,' Rosanna interjected. 'See *I* know some history. . . I could even tell you about Sir

Stamford Raffles and the fantastic way he developed the city into the giant international marketplace of south-east Asia it is today. . .a clearing house for the nation's wealth, some call it, which, considering it's only about the size of the Isle of Wight, is pretty remarkable. Do you want to hear more?'

'Not just now,' pleaded Stuart, wiping his brow. 'My head's buzzing already! Besides, I'm more interested in the medical growth of the place than anything. Apparently the money for running the first hospital came from a licence fund from the sale of opium and arrack and for operating gambling dens. Do you think we should put that idea to our management?'

'I don't think so,' Rosanna chuckled. 'But, to be serious,' she said, becoming earnest again, 'things certainly progressed pretty rapidly here after medical education started. I remember reading that surgery students were taught that lectures must be attended but surgery was to be learned standing and not sitting, from patients rather than from blackboard or print. What would you have thought of that?'

'I'd have agreed,' Stuart declared decisively. 'Anyway, let's not talk shop. If you're happy about not visiting the hospital again just now, we'll take the cable car over to Sentosa Island. I'm told that's where all the fun is.'

Rosanna brightened. 'Yes, in spite of its name meaning an isle of peace and tranquillity it's apparently full of noisy, lively activities.'

'Just what over-worked people like us need instead of lectures!' He gave her a mock frown. 'Come on, have a happy carefree holiday,' he urged, grabbing her hand again, and hurrying her along into a taxi.

'Cable Car Towers, please,' he requested, and soon they were being dropped outside the World Trade Centre right opposite the new ferry terminal on Sentosa's waterfront.

'Now that I know you're not married, and you know I'm not, we're free to fall in love. Let's find the most romantic spot on the island,' he suggested.

'Not so fast!' protested Rosanna, trying hard not to take his words seriously. 'All I want is a monorail trip around the island to get my bearings.'

'Then you'll be all set for romance?'

She had never seen him smile as attractively. Mischief enlivened his blue eyes, the deep lines on his face softened, and once more the cleft on his chin showed up flirtatiously.

Her heart raced. He put an arm about her shoulders and quite deliberately looked down into her eyes. Immediately she tensed, not knowing how to cope with the excited feelings he was arousing.

Then, without saying another word but with his arm still firmly about her, he led her into a seat on the monorail, and, disregarding all the other passengers, kissed her. . .kissed her very thoroughly, and what was even more embarrassing in Rosanna's opinion was the fact that she impulsively responded by holding up her face for yet more kisses!

The crowd behind her reacted by clapping and even cheering a little, disconcerting her and bringing her back to her senses. Self-consciously she moved away from Stuart, but he was not ready to let her go so soon.

'You're dangerous!' she accused him whisperingly. 'You know you took me by surprise, and now I'll be a laughing-stock.'

'Nonsense,' he said. 'All the world loves a lover.'

'Don't say things like that. . .you know as well as I do that I'm not a. . .a. . .what you said,' she finished lamely, unable to bring herself to repeat the word.

'Lover?' he finished for her. 'Maybe not yet, but you'd like to be if only you could throw your inhibitions to the wind—be honest now. You're all tightened up, Rosanna—try to be less rigid.'

'I don't want to be any different from the way I am and have always been,' she protested resolutely, even while finding comfort in his arms and wishing she could just stay there without having demands made upon her.

'Satisfied with being a loner, are you? Don't tell me you've never even had a boyfriend? Never had a serious relationship with anyone?'

'Have you?' she countered.

He gave her a tender squeeze. 'We're not talking about me. I've been concentrating on climbing a career ladder, and I've thought of girls as hindrances rather than assets. But I knew I'd find the right girl when I was ready for her.'

'Such conceit!' Rosanna chided, regaining her usual perkiness. 'I've been climbing a career ladder too— otherwise I wouldn't be where I am today. . .'

'On a monorail with me?'

'No,' she chuckled slightly, 'you know perfectly well what I mean.'

'Oh, yes, about you achieving a Fellowship of the Royal College of Surgeons?'

She snuggled up against him, finally unable to resist it. 'You're not in the mood to talk sense, so I won't try,' she sighed. 'You're so different when you're in our hospital. Formidable and irascible—you even scare *me* sometimes! I have to put on my special armour when you're around.'

'Is that so?' He sounded interested. 'That accounts for the deep-freeze look you give me at times.'

'I don't!' she protested.

'Oh yes, you do. Well, never mind. Look around you. See the delights we're passing. . .they say there's a wonderful insectarium here.' Rosanna shuddered. 'Also a nature walk, a deep, dark and mysterious jungle. I'd like to have you alone in there, but I suppose there'll be dozens of other tourists around.'

Stuart heaved a mock sigh and lightly rested his head against hers.

'No one would guess that we're two serious-minded surgeons, would they?' Rosanna tried to sit more circumspectly upright.

'Even surgeons have feelings, fall in love and marry,' Stuart murmured sentimentally. 'People must surely realise that fundamentally we're just as human as anyone else—so why shouldn't we be romantic? After all, the world was created out of love, and is ruled by love, no matter how much wickedness tries to make its mark.'

'You believe as I do, then, that we're each cared for by the same loving Father, no matter what or who we are?' Rosanna queried a little self-consciously, suddenly finding it important to know that she and Stuart thought alike in the things that mattered most to her.

'But of course,' he replied seriously. 'And infinitely loved—no matter how many times we let Him down. Always we're so generously forgiven—that's why we have to forgive others whatever they do against us, and why I'm forgiving you for deceiving me as you have!' With a look of great tenderness he tightened his arm about her. 'But is a monorail the right setting for such profound thought?' he questioned with a welcome touch of humour.

'You were the one to mention love,' Rosanna reminded him.

'That's because your kiss gave me an appetite for it,' he retorted cheerfully. 'Anyway, let's get off the monorail at the next of its six stations and ramble around the Coralarium probing at the colourful secrets of the sea. Apparently we can feed the turtles in the turtle pond and even handle starfish, corals and other unusual water creatures.'

'And see all the glorious colours of some endangered

species? I'd like that.' Rosanna began to blossom with interest.

'Personally I'd like to visit the maritime museum, Fort Siloso, with its underground tunnels and gun turrets, and the life-size tableaux in the Surrender Chamber depicting the signing at the end of World War Two.'

'I'm more interested in the Fountain Garden with its musical fountain playing for dancing, and the Magical Nights of Lights we've been told about.' Rosanna pointed to the notices about them in the map of Sentosa Stuart was spreading out before her.

'There you are.' Folding it and leaving the monorail, he walked with his arm around her, declaring that to let her go was to risk losing her among the crowds. 'I was right when I guessed you're as emotional as anyone else, wasn't I?' He smiled down at her. 'You like the romantic things of life—fountains, flowers, twinkling lights and all the rest, even if you try to appear more serious-minded than most girls.'

'Life's a serious business,' was Rosanna's only comment.

After the day in tropical surroundings they dined under the stars at the Rasa Sentosa Food Centre instead of returning to the hotel for the meal, then they wandered in the Fountain Garden, enchantment all around them.

'Tomorrow,' said Rosanna, 'I'd like to go shopping. We could come back to Sentosa Island and bargain our way through its stalls, buying this and that.'

'Are you in a haggling mood? One has to be quite expert at it if one wants to win the stallholders' respect. . . Otherwise they can be quite mercenary, charging the earth for things they expected you to just about halve in price!'

'I'll leave the haggling to you, then,' Rosanna declared perkily. 'It'll be good practice for when we return to our hospital and you have to try to wangle extra funds for your wards from our administrators!'

She was beginning to feel very much at home with Stuart and no longer so afraid of annoying him. He was showing many of the qualities she most admired, but whether the holiday mood was influencing him, or having a mellowing influence on them both, it was hard to tell. She gave up trying to figure it out.

Whatever or whoever was responsible for the happiness she was experiencing, she wished with all her heart that it could continue on and on for evermore.

'The days are passing like seconds, each one harbouring more contentment than the one before,' Stuart commented one evening in their second week when they were sitting down by the waterside watching junks sailing by on the smooth blue waters. 'I know we're in an idyllic situation,' he continued, 'but personally I'm finding the closeness between us growing at a most alarming rate! I want to bathe in it forever. . . How do you feel?' He smiled down at her encouragingly, but she avoided giving a direct answer.

'There's so much to see and do here that I get quite carried away,' she said instead. 'We seem to be a million miles from reality.'

'Reality being our hospital at home and the friction building up between us there?'

'You could say that.' A rather wry grimace accompanied her words.

'You don't think the feelings this holiday is stirring up will last?'

Rosanna found herself cringing. Not when you find out about my deception over Rhona and Song, she thought, allowing her guilt feelings to come to the fore again after having deliberately pushed them into the background so that she could enjoy some carefree days before she had to face up to what she feared might sour the new relationship building up between Stuart and herself.

She supposed she should be grateful for having known one perfect week even if she had no more happiness to come, she reflected miserably, completely forgetting for the moment her own maxim of not meeting anguish halfway and instead almost going the full way to meet it.

'You've retreated from me again,' Stuart eyed her perplexedly, 'gone back to fighting shy of showing emotion. One thing continues to puzzle me,' he said. 'Why *do* you call the child "son" if he isn't yours? And why should this Tang take him from you if he is?'

'You don't quite understand. I call him "son" because that's the Singaporean pronunciation of his name, although it's spelt "S-O-N-G", with a "G" at the end. I thought I'd already told you?'

'And he isn't yours? Is that the truth, Rosanna? I confess I've found it hard to credit your story, although I've tried.' The bright moonlight deepened the lines on Stuart's face into a new severity.

'Yes. I brought him over for. . .' She stopped, aghast, her tongue fortunately tripping on the name 'Rhona' before she could actually say it and give the show away. 'For a friend of mine,' she finished lamely.

'The young mother you told me about, the one whose boss wouldn't give her a chance of promotion, good reference or whatever if he knew she had a child, simply because he was against women trying to do two jobs at once? Is that why you brought the child over— you were trying to help her? The boy is really nothing to do with you? That's the truth of the matter, is it? Is it?' He sounded uncompromisingly forceful again.

Irritated by the demand in his tone, Rosanna looked straight at him and merely nodded.

His deep-set eyes narrowed shrewdly. 'Is she some-one I know?'

There was nothing she dared do but shake her head. That way at least she would not be actually speaking a lie aloud.

Both in subdued mode, and with a growing coolness between them, Stuart continued, 'Maybe I was wrong when I called you emotional. Now I'm beginning to wonder whether you even understand your own feelings. The way you were with little Song, for instance, seems to imply that you don't like children. Wouldn't you want to have some of your own?'

That was something Rosanna could answer, feeling as strongly about having children as she did. 'Of course I would. I've always wanted a family. Four at least, two girls and two boys, if possible.'

'But you'd prefer them not to have to have a father, is that it? It's men you don't like? Is that why you've never had a boyfriend?' Stuart withdrew his arm from around her shoulders. 'I've been fooling myself,' he declared. 'I thought you were capable of giving love for love, but you couldn't even give affection to little Song——'

Rosanna stood with head downcast. There seemed nothing she could say to appease him without betraying Rhona's trust, but she had to try. 'I haven't dared get too attached to him, knowing I had to hand him over to his father so soon, perhaps never to see him again,' she mumbled.

'So you tried to protect yourself from hurt, is that it?' Stuart sighed. 'Don't you think that was rather selfish of you?'

Rosanna was puzzled. Stuart seemed determined to find fault with her. They went back to the hotel barely saying a word to each other except for a mere 'Goodnight' when they parted to go to their separate rooms. It was as if a black cloud hung over them both.

It was not until she was behind her locked door that Rosanna's inter-house phone rang.

'I'm supposed to have told you that Peter Armstrong arrives tomorrow.' Stuart's voice sounded very flat and tired. 'Why he left it to me to tell you, I don't know. I'm afraid I resented his rather proprietorial message, so I tried to push it to the back of my mind, nevertheless it came more and more to the fore, eventually spoiling everything.'

After a significant pause, Rosanna saying nothing because she was lost for words, Stuart added a cursory, 'Goodnight again,' and rang off.

She threw herself across her bed and thumped her pillow, aggrieved and upset at the turn of events. Now she knew why Stuart had changed so brusquely.

But why, she asked herself, was Peter coming to Singapore?

Goaded by jealousy? Or what?

CHAPTER NINE

STUART and Rosanna were ill at ease with each other at breakfast the next day.

'Did Peter Armstrong say what time he expected to arrive?' Rosanna asked diffidently. 'Did he give any clue as to why he was coming? I didn't think he'd be up to travelling so far so soon.'

'It's surprising what love can do.' Stuart hardly raised his eyes to look at her.

'Love?' she scoffed. Then, afraid she was sounding too hard, she lapsed into silence.

'He gave the impression that you and he shared some important secret,' Stuart muttered.

Rosanna shook her head perplexedly. 'I haven't told him anything more than I've told you,' she claimed.

'He also mumbled something about your flatmate, Dr Morris, having gone to him for help.'

Startled, Rosanna gaped. 'Why would she do that?' she gulped. 'She didn't even know him!'

'No doubt he'll tell you why,' Stuart commented coldly, before adding wryly, 'If I'd had any sense I'd have suspected there was something going on between you two just from the way he tried to hold me up from joining you on the plane the day we left. Wanted to take my place, didn't he?' He paused, staring down at his full plate. 'Come to think of it,' he went on grumpily, 'he seemed just about as jealous as a cat over another's saucer of milk! Tell me, was it love at first sight for both of you, or something less creditable?'

'Now who's sounding jealous?' Rosanna sat stunned, hardly able to believe her ears. 'You surely can't think I fell in love with Peter Armstrong?'

'I've heard he's very wealthy in his own right, besides being heir to his father's millions.'

'That was a despicable thing to say!' She was furious and showed it. 'You think I can be bought? Influenced by money? Shame on you, Stuart Gainsborough!' Her fine eyes shot fire. 'It just goes to show how little you know me!'

'Which isn't exactly my fault,' he retaliated.

Pushing back her chair so abruptly that it almost overbalanced, Rosanna stood up and strode from the table, leaving her breakfast untouched. Going out through the door of the restaurant, she glanced back over her shoulder. Stuart had a daily newspaper open in front of him, seemingly engrossed in whatever it was he was reading.

Disillusioned and deeply upset, she went up to her bedroom, sought out her flight documents and studied them, half-hoping they would enable her to return to England immediately.

'Men!' she stormed aloud, disgusted with Stuart and Peter alike, then seeing she was not to get any help from her plane ticket which specified the date on which she was to use the return half, she decided to taxi to the hospital and see Tang, being in sore need of sympathy and support from someone, as well as wanting to check up on Song's health.

'He's doing very well,' Tang told her. 'No more febrile convulsions, and very happy now he is back with his beloved Aunt Nimi. You would like to see him? Well, if you can come back at noon, I will take you to share a meal with us in our home and you can see how he is for yourself.'

'In the meantime could I be permitted to look around the hospital?' asked Rosanna, loath to miss an opportunity of seeing the south-east Asia health service at work, besides being anxious to keep out of Stuart's way.

'Of course. I shall find someone to take over from me, then I shall accompany you and show you our specialities. We are proud of our links with the Scottish colleges and have good cause to be indebted to them. As far back as 1914 our first surgeon with a specialist qualification was one who came from such a college. Later two chairs of surgery were established such as in the University of Edinburgh, so as a fellow of that Royal college you can be sure of a welcome here.'

Indeed, Rosanna soon found herself so honoured, and so deeply interested in all she was told and shown, that she was able to forget for a time the aggravation caused by both by Stuart and Peter.

The scrapping of class C beds, the cheapest and most heavily subsidised of the four categories of hospital beds, was the most controversial change at the Singapore General Hospital, she found.

'We had four categories of beds,' Tang explained-while touring the wards with her. 'But the hospital was restructured last year and private companies brought in to run it. Since then things have changed. . .also there has been an increase in government subsidies.'

'Which, hopefully, will happen in our hospital system at home,' Rosanna remarked. 'Not that we have different categories of beds, although it's possible to pay for a private room if there's one available.'

'Well, our new grandeur was considered to be incompatible with the class C beds which had formerly made up the largest wards, twenty to thirty beds in each,' Tang continued. 'So it was thought that patients would prefer to pay more for better accommodation in smaller wards.'

'And do they?' Rosanna asked, interested.

'No. In any case, the decision was considered unfair to Singapore's lowest paid workers, whose nearest hospital this is. Because they could not pay the fees for A1 and B1 beds, they feared they might get inferior medical treatment, so to put minds at rest the system of class C beds is returning.'

'Sounds sensible,' Rosanna agreed thoughtfully.

'Also the hospital has managed to cut the average wait for specialist outpatient clinics from ninety minutes to forty-five, so we're heading in the right direction.' Tang drew himself up proudly to his full five foot seven inches.

'It's a lovely hospital—looks so impressive outside too, with its beautiful colonnaded entrance and the imposing clock tower above it,' remarked Rosanna.

From his receptive smile and ackowledging bow anyone would have thought Tang had built the hospital himself! 'I am very glad you like it,' he said in his precise and pleasant way. 'You think my wife will be happy to work here?'

'Oh, yes, especially as it means you can set up home together at last.' Rosanna was genuinely enthusiastic, and seeing the pleasure in Tang's kindly face she felt sure that all the trouble she had taken to help unite the little family was likely to prove well worth while.

Stuart sought her out on her return to the hotel. He made it obvious he had been waiting for her.

'Have you had lunch?' he asked solicitously, making no reference to the earlier strife between them.

'Yes.' Rosanna might have sounded abrupt, but that was because her heart had started pounding unmercifully just at the very sight of him. 'I had it with Tang and his family in their home,' she continued, looking away from him to help calm herself down. 'It was nice seeing little Song looking so fit and well and playing quite happily,' she added.

'Oh, good, I'm glad he's OK.' Stuart too seemed awkward, as if wanting to ask something yet not knowing how to put his request into words.

Possibly he's scared of being shot down in flames again, Rosanna thought impishly, glad she seemed to have the capability to shake him up mentally now and again, especially when he took up his superior stance.

Not that he could be accused of arrogance just then, indeed he was nothing if not courteously unpretentious. Having got to his feet to greet her when she arrived, he politely ushered her towards an elegantly woven wickerwork settee, pushing cushions aside to make room for them to sit side by side.

'Your cryptic remark this morning about my not knowing you struck a chord,' he told her. 'Now I'd like to remedy that omission and find out what makes you tick.'

Humour crinkled the tiny lines around his eyes as he turned his face towards her, and although determined to remain uninfluenced, Rosanna found it impossible not to melt a little towards him in spite of being sure he was making a deliberate attempt to charm her.

'What do you want to know?' she asked, slightly amused.

'Was it a good lunch?'

Surprised by the innocuous question, she was completely taken off guard. 'Very,' she smiled. '*Prata* dishes, *rojak* or *mee goreng*. . .thick yellow noodles fried with beancurd, potato, egg and peas. Or I could have chosen *poh piah*, which as no doubt *you* know,' she added in a gently mocking way, 'is a savoury roll stuffed with shredded turnips and bamboo shoots, prawns, strips of pork, and served hot.'

Neatly he parried her thrust. 'Feeling quite educated, are you? I see you were sent away well informed about local delicacies!'

She carried on quite undeterred. 'It was an excellent meal. Everything so spotlessly clean and beautifully served. Now, what else would you like to know?'

'That initial question was just to break the ice.. I want to know about you yourself.'

'Oh, no, it's your turn to reveal secrets.' Rosanna's

seeming buoyancy reflected the contentment she was beginning to feel at having him appear more at ease with her. 'What about relatives?' she asked. 'I know you have a brother because you mentioned him, but how about parents and other blood relations—have you got any?'

'My brother and I were more or less brought up by our paternal grandparents, our parents having died in a train crash when we were very young. Apart from my brother and the two nieces, his daughters, I've only the one grandfather left. He's very old and wise and declares he won't die until he's seen me safely married to a nice girl. . .which puts me in something of a quandary.'

'Why?'

'Well, I'm very fond of the old boy and don't want him to die, so it looks as if I'll have to remain a bachelor for ever.'

'You never know, he might be so happy to see you married that it'll put new life into him and he'll carry on for even more years than he would have if you hadn't!'

'Which sounds terribly Irish!' Stuart's eyebrows shot up teasingly. 'Could *you* be described as a nice girl? The sort my grandfather specifies? Could be you're putting in a plug for yourself?' His blue eyes glinted hopefully.

'Of course not!' Rosanna's colour flared. 'In any case, I'm not nice, I'm horrid and fully intend to stay that way, so you can count me out.'

He laughed. 'I take it that *you* haven't a demanding grandfather?'

'No, but I have an insistent godmother in Australia who's determined to make me a wedding dress.'

'Doesn't sound quite the same thing.' Stuart stretched his long legs out before him and dug his hands deep down into his trouser pockets.

'Relatives and godparents are all alike.' He shook a disapproving head over them. 'They forget that happy endings only happen in fairy-tales. You'd have thought the older generation would have learnt that much sense, even if only from their own experiences.'

'You're too cynical,' said Rosanna. 'My godmother was very happily married for donkey's years. She's a widow now, unfortunately, but still a great believer in romance.'

Stuart remained thoughtful, studying her. 'I wonder what you were like at school?' he reflected, screwing up his eyes as if attempting to peer beyond her into her past. 'Bright, I imagine, sporty, perhaps even gymnastically inclined, neatly built, ready to fly off the handle at the slightest provocation, nevertheless managing to stay generally well liked.'

'You flatter me! On the contrary, I was dull, plain, spindly, long-legged, and a bit of a swot, so I was inclined to keep myself to myself.'

'With long ash-blonde hair as smooth and soft as silk. . .'

'Dead straight,' Rosanna insisted, 'short, with a fringe.'

'But a peaches and cream complexion, of course.'

'With freckles!' She grimaced at the memory.

Stuart sighed and tried again, 'But eyes like the Lakes on a grey day, enchanting little green waves surfacing every now and then to tempt and tantalise?'

Refusing to take him seriously, she broke into chuckles at the image he had conjured up. 'Oh, let's go out,' she prompted, rising, Peter's message suddenly returning to sober her down and add an incentive to get away from the hotel before he could arrive.

'I haven't seen the Zoological or Botanic Gardens yet,' she pointed out, 'and who knows when I'll get another chance. Don't let's hang about here—we're wasting time.' Restlessly she walked towards the huge wide-open doors.

'Hadn't you better wait in for Peter Armstrong?' Stuart suggested, following her.

Rosanna gave him a look which spoke volumes, had he only known how to interpret it.

'You still haven't told me anything about yourself,' he reminded her while hailing another trishaw.

'I think I've told you enough.' She settled into the seat.

'It's definite that you're not married? That's the truth?' He got in beside her after directing the driver.

She nodded.

'And Song belongs to a friend of yours?'

She nodded again. 'And what's more. . .' she began.

'Yes?' Stuart turned attentively.

'I'm still waiting to try a mooncake.'

'Oh, really!' Exasperatedly he folded his arms, thumped them down against his midriff in a gesture of impatience, then signalled to the trishaw rider to stop.

'You're quite impossible, Rosanna. I've never met a girl as unpredictable as you!' he complained, after paying and dismissing the surprised Singaporean. 'But I suppose I'll have to let you have your own way. Come on, then, let's join in the festivities and cast all cares to the winds. . .will that suit you?

'And,' he continued, 'in consideration of your waist-line,' he slipped an arm around it, 'which, by the way, is ideal to hold, and so provokingly soft it demands to be squeezed now and then,' he obliged without delay, before continuing, 'as I was saying—for your figure's sake we'll indulge only on pomelos, groundnuts or some of the other festive but less fattening titbits— how will that suit you?'

But in the retaurants around colourful Chinatown, teams of chefs crispy and immaculately uniformed in black trousers, white dinner jackets and black bow-ties were out to beguile tourists into trying new varieties of mooncakes, some made with yam and lotus seed paste, others with egg yolks, red bean and durian pastes, even shredded coconut. Snow skin and pandan skin mooncakes, golden-brown mooncakes, delicately flavoured or savoury mooncakes. . .

'Too many choices!' Rosanna turned away, overwhelmed by the fascinating and mouthwatering displays set out under brilliantly designed and vibrantly coloured paper lanterns of all shapes and sizes.

'I'll have to try some mooncakes or I'll feel deprived,' she declared. 'Just about everyone seems to be either buying or eating them.'

'They have a special significance, apparently. Friends and relatives exchange delicately flavoured moon-shaped cakes to foster closer ties between man and man, or so the Singaporeans claim as they celebrate the harvest moon, which, as I think I've already told you, is thought to be at its roundest and most brilliant at about this time of the year. Some Chinese Buddhists always pray to the moon on the fifteenth day of the eighth lunar month, or so I believe.'

'Which is about now, I suppose, although I've lost count of the days recently, they seem to be simply flying past.'

'And you wish they weren't?' Stuart put in quickly. 'You're enjoying being with me—admit it now! Still, don't be so enamoured that you try to take a leaf out of the book of legends.'

'Why, what do you mean?' queried Rosanna.

'Well, from what I've read there was once a man called Hou Yi who sought perpetual youth and somehow obtained the elixir of immortality. But his wife drank it and became more and more airborne until gradually she floated right up into the palace of the moon!'

'Did she ever come back down?'

'I don't know, I haven't read that far. . .but seriously, mooncakes date back to the time when the peasants decided to revolt against tyrannical Mongol overlords. Lanterns were lit on a special day to signal the start of the uprising which led to the downfall of the Yuan dynasty. That, I suppose, is why some of the cakes are named Dynasty cakes.'

'You've certainly been studying up about them?'

Stuart looked almost bashful for a moment, then, 'Yes,' he admitted. 'Very interesting I found it, too. But actually I was hoping you'd think me very learned and knowledgeable if I came out with so many facts.'

'Hard luck!' Rosanna cradled back into the arm he still had around her. She raised her head to find him looking down at her, and for a moment the lanterns, the cakes, the colourful houses and streets were forgotten, together with all the hustling crowds. It was as if she and Stuart were alone in the world.

Then, unwillingly tearing herself away from the hope and promise in his eyes, she looked down, blushing furiously.

'Put your arm round me. . .' he was commanding gruffly, but by that time she had become aware of people milling around, of curious glances being cast their way, and, highly embarrassed, she swung away from him.

'I think you're forgetting where we are,' she told him, then for a moment feared her reminder had angered him, he straightened up so abruptly. Instead, as if coming out of a daze, he stared around.

'Great Scott!' he blurted out. 'What on earth are you doing to me, Rosanna? We can't romance in the middle of Orchard Road among all the shoppers! Quick, let's get away from this place to somewhere more private.'

And, hailing one of the ten thousand taxis plying the roads of Singapore, he ordered the driver to take

Rosanna and himself to the Jurong Bird Park, the world's largest walk-in aviary.

'You'll have nearly two thousand beautiful birds chaperoning you here,' he joked—rather self-consciously, Rosanna thought, 'and plenty of passers-by to see that I behave myself.'

And Rosanna didn't know why, but she felt very close to tears. Stuart had seemed so near and dear just minutes before, a welcome closeness building up between them. She feared the atmosphere had been destroyed, never to stand a chance of being built up again.

The rest of the day passed surprisingly happily, however, another ride on the cable-car taking them across the water to Sentosa again, where they visited the museums, a colonial fort, saw the Indonesian Rhio Islands on the horizon, then, after dining on vegetarian food served on a banana leaf, they opted to go to the Chinese Gardens in Yuan Ching Road to see the cultural spectaculars.

'I've seen the famous lion and dragon dances on TV,' remarked Rosanna, watching live performances, 'but I've never seen anything to match the magically colourful display of these intricate lanterns, to say nothing of the extravagantly fanciful costumes!'

'Fantastic!' agreed Stuart. 'Did you understand about the lanterns coming from the Suzhou Province in China?'

'No, I couldn't get even the gist of what was announced, but I loved the sight of the wonderful gossamer see-through fish vying with other creatively styled animal shapes to just about fill the sky with wavering rainbows of colours and shapes!'

'Sure, weren't they great?' An American tourist standing by enthusiastically joined in the praise. 'Shops here sell lanterns to be given as gifts to children, some of whom walk the streets in the moonlight dressed in traditional Chinese silk *samfoos*. You should just see them, they look real cute!'

'*Samfoos*?' Rosanna queried.

'Embroidered blouse or shirt with loose pants,' the lady explained, smiled, then walked on.

'We'll share the moonlight,' suggested Stuart softly, 'although I don't somehow think it'll be the children I'll be gazing at. By the way, did I tell you how much I like the little sundress you've bought? It's quite stunning. Primrose-yellow suits you.'

'As much as blue and white?' Rosanna questioned mischievously.

'Well, equally preferential to your ill-fitting white coat. Do you know, I used to think you hump-backed and double the size you should be!'

'And now?'

'I know I was right!' Grinning teasingly, Stuart dodged.

Rosanna would never have believed he could be so light-hearted, or so happy a companion. Every minute was a delight. He seemed to have dropped years.

'What a day!' She sighed with a mixture of tiredness and pleasure when at last they were back in their hotel. 'I'll never forget it as long as I live! It's been great fun.'

'And now we're alone and away from all the crowds will you let me take you in my arms, Rosanna—they've been aching and aching to hold you. . .' He reached out towards her and, with an all-embracing love softening his features, whispered, 'Dear Rosanna, could you possibly bring yourself to put an arm around me just for a moment?'

But before her instinctive shyness could allow her to make such a move a voice called, 'Hello, there!' and Peter Armstrong stepped out from the glass-walled lift as it stopped, a scowl spoiling his otherwise good looks.

'Wh—what are you doing coming here, Peter?'

Blushing from embarrassment and the shock of seeing him, Rosanna gaped at him, drawing back from Stuart.

'I had an idea something like this would happen.' Peter caught her by the elbow and turned a dismissive look towards Stuart. 'A fine way to repay our generosity!' he muttered unpleasantly, then, to Rosanna, 'I've brought a message from your friend which you won't want overheard,' he said bluntly, 'so we'll bid goodnight to Mr Gainsborough.'

Her solemn grey eyes appealed to Stuart for his understanding, but, whether deliberately or not, he apparently failed to notice, standing stony-faced and like a block.

Nonplussed as to the best way of handling the tricky situation, Rosanna said to Peter, 'You'd better come in and sit down. You're crazy to have travelled so far, you're not giving yourself a chance to get fit again, and I expect you must be very tired after the long flight.'

Then to Stuart she muttered with an air of apology, 'I'll see you in the morning,' at which he bristled, stared from her to Peter, then simply unlocked his door and disappeared into his room.

'I need a drink,' Peter claimed demandingly, swaying slightly. 'What have you got in the drinks cabinet in your room?'

'You've already had one too many, if you ask me.' Rosanna eyed him with shrewdness and concern, then, after opening her door had second thoughts and drew it to without entering her room.

'Where's your room?' she asked instead.

''T'isn't a room, it's the owner's suite. Top floor. Why, are you coming there with me? If you do I'll tell you what your friend said.'

'What Rhona said?' Rosanna echoed, surprised and anxious to hear further, urgently wanting to know if she would need to somehow prevent Peter telling Stuart the truth about Song and Tang. 'I didn't know you knew her,' she remarked, gently but insistently guiding him back into the lift.

'I didn't, not until she came to confess the intrigue. Said it was *her* son you were pretending was yours, and she was worried about him.'

His voice slurred, making it difficult for Rosanna to distinguish between his words. She had to ask him to repeat them.

'Can't it wait?' he protested, becoming disagreeable again. 'She only wanted me to send a message to her husband to find out how the boy was after the flight. Here we are. Open my door for me, will you?'

Rosanna obliged, noting how his hand was shaking, then quickly darted back to the lift, determined not to be trapped into a compromising situation with him.

'She doesn't want Stuart to know about the intrigue, so we'll have to keep away from him,' Peter called after her. 'Remember to keep away from him,' he shouted through the closing door. 'I haven't come all this way to share you!'

Inwardly distressed at the turn events were taking, Rosanna didn't wait to hear more, but as she travelled down the tubelike glass lift shaft to her own room she caught a glimpse of Stuart knocking at her door, then returning to his own room. He must be as disturbed about Peter as I am, she thought, wondering what he would have presumed at not getting an answer to his knock.

Would he have misunderstood?

She shrugged her shoulders despondently, realising that by having to keep Peter away from him she would risk losing Stuart's respect. . .and perhaps more than his respect—for hadn't he hinted at a growing love?

CHAPTER TEN

ROSANNA tossed and turned all night, snatching just a few minutes of sleep now and again, her mind worrying all the time over the new problem Peter was posing.

Could he be trusted not to reveal Rhona's secret—her secret too until Rhona had her necessary good reference and all could be explained and revealed?

Eventually giving up on the effort to get more sleep, she rose from her bed, deciding to cool herself down with a shower, but at that very moment her phone rang.

It was Peter. 'I don't feel so good,' he complained. 'Will you come up and have a look at me to see what's wrong?'

'Why not ask Stuart?' she suggested. 'He's more experienced.'

Anything, she thought, would be better than being seen going alone into Peter's room. Not even those servicing the bedrooms would realise she was simply a doctor looking in on a patient. Some might even suspect the worst!

Had she been in a happier frame of mind that idea would have amused her, whereas now it simply filled her with foreboding. Suppose Stuart heard misleading rumours, or even caught a glimpse of her coming or going from the owner's suite? What would he think?

'I thought he might be with you, but evidently not,' Peter blustered, then, changing his tone, 'Or is he?' he asked suspiciously.

So that's why you phoned, Rosanna reflected, replying with an emphatic 'No!' vexed because it seemed that he was just checking up on her. She would have said so had he given her the chance, but he went on talking.

'In any case, I didn't really want to be left alone with him in case he started asking awkward questions,' he was saying, quietening his voice down a little and speaking in such an inveigling way that it was obvious he was trying to appear conciliatory.

'He might, for instance, want to know exactly whose baby you brought over with you,' he pointed out, becoming more censuring again. '*I* know the truth now, of course, thanks to Dr Morris, but I doubt whether Stuart Gainsborough does. You're not as forthcoming as your friend was, not by a long shot!'

'I detect guilt in your silence, Rosanna,' he carried on, obviously displeased because she stayed quiet. 'You've deliberately kept the truth from him, haven't you, making loyalty to your friend your excuse? It's amazing how some people can deceive themselves when they want to enough!'

He waited as if expecting her to say something, but she remained silent, so, with a rising anger in his voice, he continued, 'You can't claim that I have the same call for confidentiality as you, because I'm sure Dr Morris must have realised that I might find myself with no alternative but to spill the beans to Dr Gainsborough.'

'Rosanna, are you listening to me?' he called down the line. 'Then say something! You and your friend between you are making my position intolerable by putting such an unfair burden on me. I've hardly slept since, it's preyed on my mind to such an extent.' He began to whine a little. 'I'm still in pain from the operation too. . . Surely you owe it to me to come up and diagnose what's wrong?' He sounded full of self-pity.

Nevertheless. . . I suppose it's the least I can do under the circumstances, Rosanna acknowledged inwardly, giving up the fight against her conscience which was insisting on reminding her that it was the duty of every doctor to put a patient's need first, even when that patient was Peter Armstrong.

'All right,' she spoke up at last and tried not to sound too reluctant, 'I'll be with you in a few moments.' Anything but happy, she replaced the receiver.

Running a comb through her hair and covering her pyjamas with the colourful silk kimono she had bought from a Chinese embroidery house just a couple of days before, she went up in the lift to the owner-suite.

To her surprise, breakfast for two was being set out on a table on the open-air terrace leading out from the sumptuous pale grey and white bedroom.

Seeing her, Peter dismissed the two waiters standing by a trolley laden with all that usually comprised a full English breakfast. . .a choice of cereals, bacon, eggs, tomatoes, mushrooms, fried bread, sausages, hot rolls, coffee, tea and an abundance of fruit of all kinds.

'Not knowing your taste in food, I ordered the lot,' he explained surprisingly brightly. 'I knew you couldn't have had time to have breakfast. If you'd prefer something more exotic to the taste—Chinese, Indian, Malay, Indonesian or Asian—you have only to say so. Our hotels are geared to supply anything,' he added proudly, 'including French fare, Italian or Mexican. . .you simply ask and the kitchen delivers.'

Rosanna smiled a little sadly, realising she had been duped into joining him when he was probably suffering from nothing more than a hangover.

Sitting under large air-cooling fans on a terrace edged by beautifully wrought white iron railings and shaded from the sun by decorative parasols should have been a pleasant experience even at that time of the morning, had Stuart been sitting opposite her, Rosanna was thinking ruefully. . .aggrieved because instead she was Peter's captive while Stuart breakfasted alone.

A very aggravating situation, especially as her heart was positively aching to be with him, to keep him company, whereas there was no thrill or satisfaction at all in being with Peter. In fact, if anything, her resentment was flaring up against him for the way he was deliberately monopolising her.

'I thought you said you were in pain?' she demurred finally, watching him making a hearty breakfast as if he were in the best of health. It was plainly obvious that he had had no medical reason for calling her to his room.

'Just my little joke,' he smirked, obviously pleased with himself for having fooled her. 'A harmless ruse. But you fell for it, didn't you! Actually, though, I'm not feeling too good.' His face lengthened. 'That's why I'm returning to England today. Eat up, you're in for a bit of a shock.'

Rosanna was immediately on guard. 'A shock? Why? What is it?' Too apprehensive to look directly at him, with a trembling finger she traced the weave of the bread basket gracing the centre of the table.

'Clever, isn't it?' Peter eyed it too. 'The basket's entirely made of spaghetti, believe it or not.' He played with it for a moment himself, seemingly lost in thought, then he began talking again.

'Well, what I've got to tell you is that I've managed to get the two last seats on today's flight home, so I've changed your booking to enable you to accompany me.' His watchful gaze never for a moment left her face.

'Caring for invalids as I'm sure you do, you wouldn't want me to be left to travel on my own again,' he went on, 'so I thought the best thing would be for you to come along with me. After all, you've had almost the full two weeks here, and we can always come back again if there's anything you've missed but would like to see. Can't say fairer than that, can I?' He smiled complacently.

By this time Rosanna was fuming inside. She had never taken kindly to being organised without being consulted first, yet there seemed little chance of doing anything but accept the present situation, especially when Peter added a subtle, 'This way there'll be no opportunity for me to give your secret away to Stuart Gainsborough. I'd hate to be the one to even accidentally reveal the deception being practised behind his back, but of course I couldn't guarantee that I wouldn't. One never knows how one would react under certain pressures.'

Controlling feelings of rising anger, 'Wouldn't you like to stay here a little longer?' she suggested, deliberately mildly so as not to risk incurring his wrath. 'There's so much to do here,' she cajoled, 'but you won't have time to even *see* anything, if you leave again so soon.'

'I've lived here half my life,' Peter replied impatiently. 'My father's business is in this part of the world, don't forget. It's all old hat to me. Besides, the reservation centre has already switched the flights. I didn't mind paying out the extra it cost and I can't have them changed back now.'

'But I still have my return ticket.'

'You're to hand that in when we go to the airport, it's all arranged.'

This is terrible, thought Rosanna, I'm being given no say in the matter at all! 'But what about Stuart?' she asked, needing to mention him, it would have been so unfair to him otherwise. 'He'll be left here on his own.'

'I'm sure he'll find ways of amusing himself for a day or two without you. Being a good doctor he'll agree that *I* have the prior right to your company, needing your help as I do. Besides,' Peter's complacent smile faded and his voice sharpened, 'I saw the way you were mooning over him last night. Sending you on holiday together wasn't such a good idea after all, especially fancying you the way I do myself.'

He began toying with the remainder of the food on his plate. 'The atmosphere of this exotic island is far too conducive to romance,' he declared. 'I couldn't have stayed here watching the two of you making up to each other! Have a heart, Rosanna.' He thumped his fist down on the table, making the dishes jump. 'And remember this. . .he wouldn't be thinking so much of you if he knew what I know, so don't force me to tell him.' There was an ominous threat in his voice. He looked down at her plate. '*You* haven't touched a thing!' he rebuked. 'Eat up, do!'

'I'm not hungry.' She got to her feet. 'I'd better go and get properly dressed,' she said, walking to the door.

'*And* packed!' He shouted the words like an order, then, even before she could fully close the door behind her, he picked up the phone again.

'Put me through to Dr Gainsborough,' he barked down to switchboard, and Rosanna waited, out of his sight but still within earshot, unhappily wondering what Stuart was to be told.

'If you're waiting for Rosanna don't,' she heard Peter say. 'She's just left my room and gone to dress. We've had breakfast, so don't hang about for her.' Then he replaced the receiver and Rosanna fled, deeply distressed.

In her room she dressed hurriedly, desperate to speak to Stuart herself to help clear up any misunderstanding, scared he might clear out of the hotel before she could get to him.

She was too late. He had already gone, leaving no message.

Despondently she returned to her room to begin

packing, throwing her clothes haphazardly into her cases. Then, using the notepaper and envelope supplied in the leather cover of the hotel brochure left standing on her dressing-table, she wrote an explanation of what was happening—in the hope that Staurt would read between the lines and realise she was accompanying Peter unwillingly, and that the change of flight reservation had not been her idea.

She had barely finished writing when Peter knocked at her door. He was dressed ready to go out. Hastily she sealed the letter into its envelope and addressed it to Stuart.

'The pageboys will strap up the cases and bring them down to the taxi,' Peter said, 'so don't bother doing anything more. We're having to leave for the airport straight away, there'll be certain formalities to be gone through, forms to fill in and sign.'

He looked around. 'You've got everything, I think,' he said, 'except this.' He picked up the envelope addressed to Stuart. 'Best to leave it with Reception,' he remarked, slipping it into a pocket of his safari-type jacket.

'I'll see to it.' Rosanna reached out for the letter.

'No need,' Peter waved her away, 'I'll hand it in with our room keys.'

Now what do I do? Rosanna asked inwardly. He'll only accuse me of not trusting him if I insist on handling the letter myself. Either that or he'll think there's more to the letter than there is! I suppose I'll have to watch to make sure he remembers to leave it with Reception.

But she was deprived of the chance, as Peter gave her the task of supervising the loading of their cases on to the taxi while he settled affairs with his father's reception clerks in their office.

There was no sign of Stuart, so no chance of speaking to him. Rosanna could feel the tears welling up inside, overflowing her heart, and more than ever before she began to realise how very much he had come to mean to her. . .but what could she do about it?

With misting eyes she searched as far as she was able, all the time hoping and praying to see his tall figure towering above the passing crowds and coming towards her.

What she longed to do was to explain to him, telling him the truth about everything, but after the unpleasantness of the evening before when Peter arrived so unexpectedly, dismissing him so arrogantly, and the misapprehension he must have suffered when he found her missing from her bedroom later—well, the relationship between them might possibly have been damaged beyond repair. It was a chastening thought. She gulped, fighting sadness and heartache such as she had never known before.

As they came out of the hotel Peter hustled her into the taxi.

'I'd like to say goodbye to Song and his father,' she protested. 'It will seem odd to the family if I go away without seeing them.'

'There's no time,' Peter insisted.

She tried another stratagem. 'But Dr Morris will want to hear how her son was when I left.'

'She knows he was all right when I contacted her husband by fax, and we can always repeat the process when we get back to England, or even phone from the airport.'

He has an answer to everything, Rosanna thought, despairing of ever getting him to do what she wanted. Things had gone badly wrong, the so-called holiday having been completely spoilt, and in a way, she thought, it was her fault.

'Time to board the plane,' Peter reminded her at long last, all the flight formalities having been completed and a tour of the new terminal undertaken, last-minute shopping filling up the rest of the waiting period.

'I think you've been deliberately keeping me on my feet!' he groused, just as if it had not been his own fault. 'Anyway, I can't possibly walk another step. This new second-floor departure hall might be acclaimed for the natural light its high, terraced-in-progression ceiling allows to filter through, but it does nothing for a body as sore as mine. You'd better see about getting me a wheelchair. I don't need one of those with elevating foot rests, the ordinary type will do. I'll just put up with the pain in my operation scar.'

Rosanna tried not to feel offended by the implied criticism of the difficult operation she and Stuart had performed so successfully, but, realising Peter was enjoying putting on the mantle of a martyr, she let his derogatory remark pass.

Staring around, she remarked that there were no wheelchairs as far as she could see.

'Of course there must be wheelchairs,' said Peter, annoyed. 'Changi Airport has everything air travellers could need. Call one of the "meet and assist" people over—we should have arranged to have their help from the start. Look, there's one, they all wear those bright yellow jackets.'

'We'll put him in an airport buggy,' the charming Singaporean girl replied when Rosanna turned to her for assistance. 'They look like normal wheelchairs except that they change into an aisle chair when their large main wheels are detached, becoming so narrow that it's easy to manoeuvre them along the aisle inside the plane. Ordinary wheelchairs would get stuck, as I know from my own experience!' She laughed.

'Why, what happened?' Rosanna asked.

'The passenger, a very heavy man, collapsed the chair and landed on the floor! Passengers laughed and the man was not hurt, but me, I nearly died!' The girl tried to look serious, but meeting Rosanna's amused smile, joined her in a chuckle.

'Well, don't let the chair collapse under *me*,' chided Peter, warily installing himself into the airport buggy. 'I assure you I wouldn't find it at all funny.'

The girls looked at each other, grinned conspiratorially behind his back, then parted, as another passenger beckoned for meet-and-assist service.

'I hope he's not just wanting me to carry his hand luggage for him, that's not what we're here for,' the cheerful young Singaporean whispered to Rosanna as they parted. 'We want to help the *really* needy. We wouldn't have time to help everyone.'

'What's all the nattering?' Peter twisted around to ask.

'Nothing much,' Rosanna assured him. 'But, Peter, are you sure you're justified in taking over a wheelchair? You're quite capable of walking, you know, and there might be someone really in need of one. . .an amputee, perhaps?'

'Oh, just get me along to the plane, then the chair can be brought back,' he snapped. 'I can't understand why so many are in use already.'

'Because some genuinely handicapped people need them, I suppose,' Rosanna retorted, then, unable to help herself, 'You know, you're very disagreeable and selfish,' she added exasperatedly, wheeling him along. 'When you were a patient in hospital you were very different, we all thought how pleasant you were.'

He remained quiet after that reprimand, so Rosanna bit back further reproaches, sure she must already have stunned him by speaking out as she had; however, she was beyond caring.

Everything seemed to be going wrong for her. She was flying away from the one person she wanted to be with, and nothing else seemed to matter.

It would be a great relief to get back to work, she

decided, hoping that then perhaps she could forget herself in sorting out other people's problems.

In complete contrast to the outward journey, she had little to do but sit and think all the homeward miles away. It was a dull journey. She missed little Song, but more than anything she missed Stuart.

Fortunately Peter dozed frequently and she was able to pretend to be asleep herself whenever he was fully awake. In that way and with the help of appearing to listen to the in-flight music, or apparently lose herself in a magazine, book or film, she managed to pass the long hours without finding everything becoming too much of a hassle.

Finally the plane approached England, and Rosanna's heart rose at the distant view of misty green fields beyond an azure sea dotted by white sails. England, where she would be able to say goodbye to Peter!

Likening her rising spirits to those of prisoners completing their sentences and going out to enjoy freedom, she beamed around at the other passengers, not caring if they did think her a little mad!

'It's a bright Tuesday morning. Time to rejoice!' she declared after a while, elbowing Peter. 'Wake up! The plane's circling Manchester Airport now. We're about to land—isn't it wonderful?'

Peter opened one eye and peered towards a window while he fastened his seatbelt. 'It's raining,' he observed dully. 'I can't see there's anything to be so pleased about!' He studied his wrist watch. 'This has to go back eight hours now. Think how tired we'll be by this evening!'

'So now we have eight hours *plus* a whole lifetime ahead of us?' Rosanna responded brightly, full of joy because she was about to regain her independence.

'*You* might have a long life ahead, but I'm not so sure I have,' Peter said gloomily. 'I'm anything but fit.

Anyway, are you coming to my home with me? I'd like to go straight there. I need to rest. Not only that, but my father will be anxious to hear how things went during the holiday.'

I wouldn't be able to tell him the truth, Rosanna thought, so what would be the point in going? Besides, she had had enough of Peter's company. The door to complete freedom was opening, and not for anything in the world was she going to be the one to slam it shut again.

'I'd prefer to get back to work straight away,' she said, making the only excuse she could think up. 'I can save two days' holiday time if I do.'

Peter shrugged. 'I would have thought you'd prefer to pay your respects to my father, after all he's done for you, and surely there's a danger you'll make mistakes and wrong decisions in your work, being jet-lagged? I'm glad you won't be operating on me—you look as tired as I feel. As for me, I think I'll go to bed as soon as I get home.'

'Good idea.' Rosanna brightened at the ease with which she was getting rid of him. 'Neither of us is in any mood to talk, so I'll come and see your father when we're both feeling more rested. OK?'

She quickly repacked her hand luggage and waited for Peter to collect up his own belongings. 'Shouldn't you be putting on something warmer than that short-sleeved jacket?' she asked, adding a wry, 'This isn't the island of eternal summer, you know; when you leave this air-conditioned plane you'll find it's near winter in Manchester!'

'Oh, I suppose I'm in no condition to take risks.' Peter threw off the cotton jacket and drawing a thick sweater from his flight bag, pulled it on over his head. Thinking to speed up their departure from the aircraft, Rosanna picked up his jacket, meaning to fold it ready for him to pack it away.

Her letter to Stuart half fell out of the pocket. She stared, horrified. Peter made an attempt to hide it, but was not quick enough.

'You didn't leave it with Reception as you promised!' she accused, taking it back into her own possession.

'I meant to, but I had other things to do,' he excused himself. 'Anyway, you'll be seeing him soon enough, so you can tell him personally whatever it was you wrote in the letter.'

'That's hardly the point!' Rosanna found herself close to tears.

'No good crying over spilt milk,' Peter quoted unfeelingly. 'Come on, let's get off the plane—I'm desperate to get home. Are you coming with me or aren't you?'

Rosanna shook her head. 'I told you, no,' she repeated wearily, much too miserable about the unde-livered letter and the possible consequences to say more than she had to.

And, 'Just drop me off at the hospital, please,' was all she was able to add when the Armstrong limousine came to collect Peter and herself.

She was warmly welcomed back at the hospital, however, which helped raise her spirits, although Sister Mills strove to put her straight back to work.

'We've been rushed off our feet, inundated with emergencies,' panted the buxom sister. 'Never been more short-staffed, either—we couldn't get a locum. Did you have a good holiday?' Then without as much as a pause for Rosanna to get a word in, she added, 'Oh, good, tell me all about it when things slacken off, that's if they ever do!'

'You'll find a clean white coat in your office,' she advised over her shoulder as she rushed around. 'Our waiting time's beyond acceptable limits, we must get it down.'

She picked a card from the doctors' box as she passed it.

'This is about the eighteen-month-old girl due to be seen next.' She looked down at the particulars written on the card. 'It's an electric burn. The mother's terribly distressed.'

'I'll do the best I can, but I'm probably quite a bit dopey after the long flight,' Rosanna replied. 'Can you brief me a little more about the child?'

'A staff nurse is waiting in the cubicle with her—I haven't had time to go in there myself. Yes? What did you want to know?' Breaking off, Sister Mills turned to answer a query from a new male staff nurse wanting her advice.

So Rosanna hurried along to the cubicle to question the child's mother herself, fishing the full story out of her as quickly and kindly as she could.

'I'm always so careful,' sobbed the young mother. 'Very safety-conscious, that's why I had guards put over the electric sockets, but Kylie found some keys. . .' she hiccuped and shed fresh tears before continuing '. . .and I can only think she thought the socket was a keyhole and somehow managed to push a key into it. . .oh, she could have been killed, couldn't she!'

'But she wasn't, she's here safe and sound,' Rosanna reminded her reassuringly. 'So then what happened?'

'I heard her crying and ran in. She was sitting on the floor by the socket and nursing her arm, so I guessed what had happened.'

'Well, please undress her,' said Rosanna. 'I'm sure she'd be happier to have you do it rather than me. I want to see where the exit burn is.'

'Exit burn?' The child's mother looked up, puzzled.

'That's where the electricity leaves the body to go to earth,' explained Rosanna, then, turning, she asked the staff nurse to organise an ECG.

'Which is just to make sure there isn't a heart rhythm

disturbance,' she told the young mother when the staff nurse returned from the phone bringing a student with her to be shown how to do the burns dressing.

'I'm going to refer little Kylie to the paediatricians to see whether it's necessary to keep her in for observation,' Rosanna continued, deliberately keeping the distressed mother fully informed in order to build up her confidence and help her regain her composure. 'But whether or not she has to stay in,' she added in her soothing yet highly professional bedside manner, 'she'll need to come and have her burn re-dressed tomorrow.' She studied the small child reflectively. 'I don't think it'll be necessary for the plastic surgeons to become involved. Anyway, we'll see.'

Then with a cheering smile she left the staff nurse to see that Kylie had all the necessary treatment, and went on to the next patient, a young man who had stuck four needles into his knee.

'What on earth did you want to do that for?' Rosanna asked, losing patience because the injury had been self-inflicted and not accidental.

'Well, I'd been reading about acupuncture, so I thought I'd try it out on myself,' he replied sullenly.

'But why on your knee?' Rosanna wanted to know, studying his X-ray film.

The young man turned his head away, refusing to answer.

The attendant staff nurse drew Rosanna aisde. 'I can tell you why,' she murmured out of his hearing. 'He told me he'd had some psychiatric treatment on his head, and having read that the knee's a pressure point, he thought he'd save himself from having any more!'

'Well, well,' said Rosanna, 'we get all sorts, don't we!' Then, aware of being lacking in sympathy, she realised how very tired she must be to have spoken in such a derogatory way about a patient.

So she called one of the casualty officers over. 'I

think you'll have to draw out those needles,' she said, 'then the patient had better be referred to the on-call psychiatric liaison officer for some counselling. I don't feel capable of doing much good here.'

'You've just had a long flight, haven't you? Perhaps you're jet-lagged?' a staff nurse suggested compassionately.

'I didn't think I would be.' Rosanna ran a hand through her short hair, uncaringly leaving it all messed up. 'After all, I did all the right things, those advocated by medical professors who should know the best way to avoid it. I ate very little, didn't drink alcohol or fizz because of fluid loss—knowing humidity is necessarily low on aircraft because of the weight of water needed for it—and I even avoided caffeine. The only thing I didn't do that some experts advise was wear an eye mask to combat personality change! Whether I've changed for the better or for the worse, I don't know— no doubt you'll all find out soon enough!'

The staff nurse laughed, and Rosanna went off to tell Sister Mills that come what may she would *have* to have a doze before being capable of doing any more work.

'Not being due back on duty for another two days I feel less guilty about it than I would otherwise, but after catching up on a bit of sleep I'll be able to do twice as much, twice as well, than if I stay on now,' she declared.

'You know best,' said Sister, mellowing. 'I was trying to pass the buck, wasn't I? As no doubt you've noticed, I tend to get flustered when the cards pile up in the boxes. I probably would have prodded the Minister of Health into helping out, had I had the chance!'

'Which would have proved interesting, considering he isn't a doctor!' Rosanna quipped feebly, although actually managing to raise a smile. It faded, however, when she passed the glamorous Alexa sitting typing in

Stuart's office, for above the desk, in the position of honour, was a postcard of Singapore.

'Hello,' said Alexa, turning round at the sound of footsteps, 'you're back early. . .but that's funny,' her normally smooth brow actually furrowed, 'Stuart's still out in Singapore. . .isn't he?'

'Was that from Stuart?' Rosanna couldn't help asking, pointedly nodding towards the postcard and thinking it strange he had never mentioned sending one, although it must have been posted quite early on in their holiday.

'Oh yes, wasn't that sweet of him?' Alexa took it down, turned it over. 'More than friendly too! I'm looking forward to the dinner date he mentions.' She read the card over to herself, a satisfied smile crossing her beautifully made-up face, but she made no attempt to let Rosanna see what Stuart had written.

Not that I'd want to read it anyway, thought Rosanna crossly, walking off along the corridor towards the doctors' residences, dragging her cases with her. Dragging her feet rather despondently too, sure her life was becoming something of a mess and all because she had let pity sway her in her dealings with Peter Armstrong.

Yet did she want to allow herself to become callous and hard-hearted? No, she assured herself wryly, although, come to think of it, in Peter's case it might serve a purpose!

Back in her flat, without attempting to unpack anything, she kicked off her shoes and threw herself across her bed, still debating whether or not it would be a good thing to deliberately toughen up a little. Towards Peter, yes, she decided, but—towards Stuart?

Before making up her mind one way or the other she had to answer the front door, as the bell was ringing insistently.

'Heard you were back,' said Kevin, stepping inside

the little hallway. 'I also heard you've left Stuart behind. Is that right?'

'I returned two days early,' she replied, slipping her feet into slippers.

'Quarrelled with him again?' Hope began to shine in Kevin's eyes.

'Peter Armstrong came out to bring me back,' she explained.

'Whew, he has a nerve! Wants you for himself, does he?'

'I'm exhausted, Kevin,' she sighed. 'I'm not really wanting to talk about it just now.'

Kevin smiled back. 'You look beautiful to me whether you're tired or full of life.'

'Oh, Kevin, you certainly know how to make a girl feel special! Thanks for being a tonic.'

'I can see you're not up to coming out, though,' Kevin moved to the kitchen and put the kettle on to boil, 'so I'll make you a cuppa and let you get to bed. I won't worry you with any more questions.'

She smiled a grateful thanks for his understanding.

'So your flatmate's going off to Singapore as soon as Stuart gets back.' Kevin remarked while making the tea. 'And there's just one question I must ask. . .any biscuits anywhere?'

'In that tin over there.' Rosanna jerked her head towards it while collapsing down on to one of the kitchen chairs by the table. 'I had no idea Rhona would be leaving so soon.'

'It's only natural for her to want to be reunited with her husband and son as quickly as possible,' said Kevin, surprising her by knowing about them. 'She's taking it for granted she'll get a good reference from Stuart. Do you think she will?'

Rosanna nodded. 'Yes, I think we've been misjudging him. He's a fair man, not one to let personal prejudices affect other people's lives. I've been assured of that. We had no right to deceive him as we did,' she added a little shamefacedly.

'He knows the truth now? You told him?'

'No, I'd promised not to, but I expect he's guessed. He's not stupid, he'll have put two and two together, How did *you* find out?'

'Rhona told me. She also told Peter, I believe. Anyway, it couldn't have remained a secret for much longer. Well, drink up and get your head down on your pillow. I'm off now. And, Rosanna,' Kevin looked back from the kitchen doorway, 'don't be so scared of losing Stuart to Alexa.'

'Are my feelings so transparent?' she said ruefully.

Kevin smiled. 'Love has that effect—I should know, I've been in and out of love so often. I'm not like you, a strictly one-man girl!'

'I should hope not!' Tired as she was, Rosanna was unable to suppress a giggle at his words.

His colour heightened. 'Oh, you know jolly well what I mean! I'm not a *one-girl man*—there, is that better?' Then with a telling look he added, 'But I might well have been, had *you* encouraged me.' And with that, he left.

Her spirits partially lifted, Rosanna stumbled into her bedroom, flung herself across her bed, then— almost before her head hit the pillow—fell asleep.

CHAPTER ELEVEN

AWAKENING refreshed, Rosanna changed out of her sleep-creased skirt and sweater and went along to Casualty, calling in at the canteen on the way for a quick snack, contrasting it in her mind with the hotel meals in Singapore, but knowing those meals would not have been conducive to indulging in hard work afterwards.

She wanted to work hard, to take her mind off Alexa, and Peter, and even Stuart. As yet there had been no time or opportunity to see Rhona, or Kevin, who might perhaps have provided a little light relief to the problems still at the back of her mind.

Her first patient came in with a noble smile but a tale of woe. 'I was putting up a shelf, accidentally drilled through an electric cable, escaped without mishap but with an increased awareness of safety risks, so I put up a smoke alarm and while doing so I fell off my step-ladder and I think I've broken my wrist!' The forty-year-old spoke without the slightest sign of self-pity, his air one of amused self-condemnation instead.

'I think you're right, it is broken.' Rosanna examined it carefully, then sent him off for an X-ray to see exactly what and where the damage was, at the same time wishing all patients could be as pleasant and uncomplaining as he was.

How differently Peter was reacting to his accident, she reflected, immediately chiding herself for letting him come to mind when she was struggling so hard to forget everything but her work.

Afterwards, walking past the cubicles in the short-stay ward in order to collect another card from the doctors' box, she was startled by a loud, querulous but very joyful cry of 'Hello, Felicity, how nice of you to come!'

Glancing curiously around, she saw a little old lady sitting up in bed smilingly holding out her hand in greeting.

Walking over to her, Rosanna gave the tiny wizened hand a gentle shake. 'I'm afraid I'm not Felicity,' she said, 'but hello all the same!' then, smiling, she walked on.

But when passing the same cubicle on her way back she found herself once again being greeted by the welcoming, 'Hello, Felicity, how nice of you to come!'

As this happened every time she went by, and she was unable to keep stopping when she had so many patients to see to, finally she was forced to find another route to the doctors' box. To her surprise the delighted cry was still being repeated time after time, much to everyone's amusement.

'To her, every one of us is Felicity,' remarked a giggly young student nurse.

'Yes, apparently we all appear one and the same to her,' a staff nurse joined in, 'including the male nurses and porters! She doesn't differentiate between any of us, no matter how we're dressed, in fact the dear old soul loves us all equally, which makes us feel good, cheers the whole place up.'

'Why is she here?' Rosanna asked.

'Fell down, and it was thought her hip might have broken—causing the fall—or it could have been broken by it. However, the hip's OK, fortunately. She's been living on her own, but the social workers have discovered a niece who's willing to take her into her own home and look after her, but because she'll need to buy another bed first, she can't take her until tomorrow, so we're keeping her in overnight.'

'I hope she won't be too unhappy at being moved from her own home,' Rosanna mused thoughtfully.

'I'm sure she won't be, not if she's allowed to call the niece Felicity,' the staff nurse assured her. 'The niece's name is Sarah, actually, but she says she won't mind. She seems very understanding and co-operative.'

'She'll need to be,' remarked Rosanna. 'Not everyone would take kindly to being called by the wrong name all the time. . .or to having to shake hands every moment or two!'

Grimacing facetiously, she rubbed her own right wrist as if it still suffered from being shaken so often, then, becoming more serious again, she took another card from the box and, skirting the cubicles, sought the next patient and found him—a lively two-year-old who was strutting around proudly carrying a vomit bowl on his head, while a young woman watched.

'Prepared for the worst, is he?' Rosanna commented humorously, then looking down at his casualty card, 'I see he drank quite a lot of his cough medicine. Are you his mother?'

'Brought me the empty bottle, he did, licking his lips and saying "Lully, Mummy, lully!"' the young woman told her. 'I thought I'd put it out of his reach. Nearly had a fit, didn't I! We've been trying to make him sick ever since, but nothing's worked, not even that horrible. . .epec. . .ipeccec. . . I'm not sure how to pronounce it. . .'

'Ipecacuanha?'

'Yes, that's the stuff. . .even that hasn't made him throw up.'

'Must have a cast-iron tummy,' Rosanna concluded lightly, taking the child on to her knee but finding it impossible to prevent him wriggling off. 'He's lively enough,' she said, giving up and letting him go. 'He doesn't seem to have come to any harm, fortunately, but watch out that he doesn't become unusually drowsy. Let us know immediately if he does. Right?'

A three-year-old was the next patient. He had fallen off a bench and was not using one of his arms.

'He doesn't seem to be in pain,' his father told Rosanna.

'Does your arm hurt?' she asked the child.

He shook his head.

'All the same, I think he's broken it,' Rosanna told the father after examining the limb. 'He'll need to have an X-ray.' She patted the boy's curly head. 'You're going to have a photo taken,' she said. 'Smile when you do, won't you?'

The boy's round blue eyes looked up at her, 'Yeth,' he lisped, 'and I'll give you one of my photos.'

'Oh, thank you!' Rosanna beamed at him, again impressed by the courageous example some children set, even when faced by the unknown.

'I'm going off duty now,' Sister Mills popped her head round into Rosanna's office to announce. 'Things are easing up a little, and I've already been on longer than I should.'

She had no sooner gone than an ambulance arrived bringing in an elderly lady who had collapsed in the town's shopping precinct and almost died, saved at the last moment by the expert resuscitation of the ambulance men.

'I'm not afraid of dying,' she told Rosanna while she was being examined. 'I got near it, didn't I? It wasn't scaring. There was this bright light coming towards me. Do you think it was Jesus? I'd like to have gone to Heaven. I know I don't *deserve* to, but none of us could, could we? It's a good job Jesus deserved it for us—we'd never make it on our own. I was almost there, wasn't I? I wish I'd been allowed to go on.' A tear trickled down her cheek. 'Now I've got to go through it all over again to get to Him!'

'I wish we all had your faith,' Rosanna said enviously. 'It would make life so much easier all round. But I don't think you'll be going to Heaven just yet, you've recovered so well. I expect God has some job He wants you to do for Him first, so let's hope, with the treatment we'll give you here and preventive medicine to keep up the good work afterwards, you'll be fit to do it—and what's more, will probably outlive us all!'

If only I could sort myself out as easily as I sort out other's troubles, she thought afterwards, finding herself still unable to resist wondering where Stuart was, what he was doing, and how he had reacted to her apparent desertion.

She was soon to find out. He was on her doorstep two evenings later.

'A dozen red roses,' he said, thrusting them towards her.

Her heart jumped for joy as she bent her head over them, inhaling their fragrance. 'Thank you very much—they're lovely,' she said, stepping back meaning to invite him into the little lounge, but before she could. . .

'Oh, they're not from me,' he declared hastily. 'They were left in my office, and as it seemed certain they'd be neglected overnight I brought them round for you to see to. It didn't seem as if anyone else would bother.'

No, thought Rosanna a little peevishly, Alexa would have left them to die from want of water in case they were for me from you. She drew out a little gift envelope from among the roses.

'For you from Peter Armstrong?' Stuart suggested gravely, eyebrows raised.

'I don't know, I don't like to open it.'

'Not in front of me, is that it? Well, if you want privacy, I'll be off.'

All the light faded from Rosanna's eyes. 'Are you

implying that Peter and I share some intimate secret?' she asked.

Stuart shrugged his wide shoulders. 'Well, don't you? You left me for him, didn't you?' He growled a little. 'What I'm trying to point out is that by leaving me in Singapore and going off with him you made it patently clear that something pretty serious was happening between the two of you.'

'It takes two to make a romance,' Rosanna pointed out, openly offended. 'Anyway, don't let's argue on the doorstep—come inside.'

'Who says we're arguing?' He stood firm. 'No, I won't come in.' His expression hardened. 'I don't poach on other men's preserves,' he declared sternly, head held high.

'Well!' Rosanna saw red at that, flung the door wide open and walked off into her kitchen.

After a second's hesitation, Stuart followed.

'Look,' she began, facing him after putting the roses in a jug of water, 'you might as well know that I didn't *want* to leave Singapore with Peter Armstrong, but he gave me no alternative, having changed my flight without my knowledge. I did my best to find you to explain matters, but you'd already left the hotel.'

'And you couldn't be bothered to write me a note explaining what was happening?' He looked every bit as angry as she felt, she noticed, her temper coming to the boil again.

'Don't jump down my throat!' she almost shouted in retaliation. 'I *did* bother. At least, I wrote you a note, but Peter picked it up, saying he'd leave it in Reception for you. . .only he didn't.' Calming slightly, she blinked rapidly to clear her unhappy eyes. 'I found it when we were in the plane. It more or less fell out of his pocket. I kept it as evidence, being pretty sure I wouldn't be believed by you. . .knowing your suspicious nature!'

'Me, suspicious?' he echoed, openly outraged by the very suggestion, so she disappeared into her bedroom to come out with an unopened envelope in her hand.

She handed it to him. 'I never had the heart to reopen it,' she muttered.

Stuart had no such qualms. Rapidly he slid a thumb along under the sealed flap, then stood reading the letter while she watched his face, wondering what his reaction would be.

For a few seconds he said nothing, then. . . 'This puts a different complexion on things,' he made an obvious effort to sound apologetic. 'I wonder why Peter Armstrong didn't leave it for me. Did he genuinely forget—or was it a deliberate slip of the memory? What do *you* think?'

'I don't know,' Rosanna mumbled miserably, glad nevertheless to perceive the change in Stuart's attitude. 'He seems so sure he has some prior right over me, so I don't think he's too happy about you.' She coloured a little. 'I don't know why that should be,' she added lamely.

'I do—it's obvious. Well, thanks for the explanation.' He glanced at his wristwatch. 'I've got to go.' he said, 'but before I do, can we kiss and make up?'

The offhand way he said it was enough to put Rosanna's back up again, even make her remember Alexa's words. Vexed, she wondered whether his hurry was because he was taking *her* out to dinner—as she had implied was his intention?

She shook her head. 'No kissing,' she decreed, then, bracing herself to come out into the open about her objection, 'You'd better hurry,' she said loftily. 'You've got a date with your secretary, I believe. And Mr Gainsborough,' she added in an austere, formal way, '*you* would do well to remember in future that *I* do not poach on other girls' preserves!'

There, that should teach him, she gloated.

'Wow!' Looking down at her, completely flabbergasted, he followed as with prim dignity she led him back to the front door.

Short as she was compared with him, she seemed to grow in stature as she added reprimandingly while opening the front door, 'You should have known I wouldn't have acted in the discreditable way you apparently presumed I had—not of my own free will, anyway. So goodnight now—perhaps goodbye.'

Still apparently bemused, nevertheless he made one last stand. 'I object to being pushed out like this,' he declared with renewed vigour.

'I'm afraid you have no choice in the matter, Mr Gainsborough,' Rosanna said steadily. 'I'm going to bed. Life has been particularly exhausting lately.' And closing the door behind him, she stood leaning up against it trying to regain enough equanimity to stop her wholesale trembling.

Shutting him out had been one of the hardest things she had ever done, while her dismissive last words had had to be torn from her heart.

Regrets crowded in on her. She could have had his kiss. . .would it be given to Alexa instead? Miserably she supposed so. After all, she had practically thrown the girl into his arms!

What must Stuart be thinking of her now?

Before she had the energy to undress and get to bed, Kevin called almost as if to tell her. 'I don't know what you did to our formidable consultant surgeon tonight,' he said, 'but I've heard he's storming around the various hospital departments picking on this, picking on that—anyone would think he owns the joint! As for the staff, we're expecting wholesale resignations to flood in, he's putting so many backs up. I tell you, Rosanna, there's a rebellion brewing! Hurricane force twelve at the very least, and the funny thing is, it's all come to a head so suddenly!'

Rosanna smiled, relief tinged with guilt. Guilt in case her outburst had caused the tempestuous repercussions the staff were witnessing, relief because while still in hospital Stuart obviously could not be out wining and dining Alexa!

'However, putting Stuart aside—as many of us would love to do—what about coming out to dinner with me to tell me all your news?' Kevin suggested. 'How *was* Singapore, for instance?'

'Fantastic!' Rosanna brightened by the moment, as she usually did under Kevin's influence. 'All right, I'll come. I was going to have an early night, but,' she shrugged, 'I'm not really ready for oblivion yet! I'd better leave a note for Rhona, though. I haven't seen her yet, she's been on some course or other. She should be back later on tonight.'

'Then come out now, just as you are. Stuart's been round already, hasn't he? When I came in I could tell your feathers had been ruffled!'

'I don't know why he went over to the hospital,' she called out as she fetched her jacket and handbag from her bedroom, 'I thought he was supposed to be dining with his beloved secretary?'

'Thought, or feared?' Kevin asked shrewdly. 'Anyway, pull your claws back,' he glanced chidingly at her. 'He's entitled to take her out if he wants to. He isn't tied to you. . .well, not yet, anyway.' Then he added quietly, 'Much as you'd like him to be. . .and that's the truth, the whole truth and nothing but the truth, isn't it Rosanna?'

She had no recourse but to pretend she hadn't heard. All the same. she found it impossible not to harp on the subject of Stuart. 'He can't have had much sleep,' she remarked. 'He must be jet-lagged, surely?'

'Now you're trying to make excuses for him,' Kevin sighed. 'Can't we talk about *me* for a change?' He led her to his vintage car. 'It still goes,' he promised, trying to open its door, then giving up and lifting her inside on to the passenger seat. 'Where would you like to go? Somewhere exotic, or have you had your fill of bizarre allure lately? Oh, sorry, I didn't mean to allude to Alexa again so soon!'

Rosanna laughed, she couldn't help it.

The evening remained happy. Kevin was always easy to chat to, and being Irish had a whole fund of amusing stories to tell.

'You'd have laughed with the rest of us one day last week when you were away,' he said. 'There was a chap in Casualty who needed a tetanus injection but wasn't very keen on having one. His language contained words even I had never heard before, but one could tell what sort they were. Then when the needle went in he seemed lost for an appropriate expletive, so what do you think Sister Mills resorted to? With a primly reproving air she insisted, "*Sugar* is the word we use here!"'

Rosanna grinned. 'And what happened?'

'There was dead silence for a moment, then a burst of laughter, everyone joining in—even the chap himself!'

'I had a young boy in today who'd trapped his finger in one of the holes in a light plastic ball—you know the sort?' Rosanna reminisced.

Kevin nodded. 'The type children are given to play with indoors because they can't do much damage to the furniture?'

'Yes. Well, to keep the boy's mind occupied while I cut the ball away from his finger—the plastic had cut into it a bit and there was some swelling and bleeding— I asked him what he wanted for Christmas.'

'A bit too early to talk about Christmas, surely?'

'It was all I could think of at the time. Anyway, he started crying, so I asked why—was the finger hurting all that much?'

'"No," he sobbed, then went on to tell me that although he'd been good and done all he was told to do last Christmas, his parents didn't give him presents as they'd promised. . .only Father Christmas gave him presents!'

'Just shows you what kids think,' Kevin reflected. 'So what did you say?'

'I told him that his mum and dad had given Father Christmas the money to buy the presents—explained that he's a saint and lives in Heaven where money isn't made or used, so the only way he can buy the things children want to play with on earth is to have the money given to him by their parents, uncles, aunts or friends.'

'Not much of an answer, I know,' Rosanna added wryly, 'but it seemed to satisfy him, although when I went on to tell him that some children don't have anyone to give Father Christmas the money to buy presents for them, tears rained down his cheeks on their behalf! An emotional little boy, I think.'

'Can't win, can you!' Kevin chuckled wryly. 'But maybe the pity you stirred up in him might result in him helping others less fortunate than himself one day. One never knows.'

'An optimist talking!' Rosanna smiled at him. 'Actually, I don't think I'm much good at sermonising!' she pulled a face at her inability to preach. 'I seem better able to pull people down rather than build them up.'

'Now you're fishing for compliments,' Kevin quipped. 'But let's cut out philosophy and have something we can digest instead.' He parked the car by a hotel. 'This place is pretty good usually,' he told her.

The food was excellent, his company exhilarating, and all in all Rosanna should have thoroughly enjoyed herself. The trouble was, she simply could not forget Stuart, as Kevin was evidently aware, for his eyes, behind their encouraging smiles, held a lurking wistfulness.

He drove her back to her accommodation after the meal.

'I won't come in,' he said, 'or I might deprive you of your beauty sleep. And he made no attempt to kiss her or even put his arm round her.

Which was just as well, as it turned out, because Stuart was walking towards another of the residential blocks, and he was not alone. There was a girl with him.

'Thanks for the lovely evening and dinner, Kev,' Rosanna said hastily, almost tumbling out of the car in her haste to get into her flat and out of sight of the couple strolling over the lawn.

'Don't worry,' Kevin smiled understandingly, nodding back towards Stuart, 'he hasn't seen you yet.'

He wouldn't care even if he had, Rosanna only just stopped herself replying, bitterness in her voice. Instead, feeling sorry for Kevin, she turned back, bent towards him, planted a swift kiss on his cheek with a whispered, 'Goodnight, God bless, and thanks,' before forcing herself to walk tall to her front door.

She had to salvage her pride, for, without having intended him to notice, she knew Stuart must have seen the kiss, would have remembered too how she had refused his, and might even recall her declaring herself too tired for anything but an early night. Yet here she was, coming back late with Kevin! To say nothing of having red roses sent to her by Peter!

Trust me to mess things up completely, she scolded herself after getting into her bed that night, then suddenly she chuckled, her sense of humour making a comeback.

She was realising that if Stuart thought of her at all he must be wondering which of three men she was after. . . Peter for his money, Kevin for his lively companionship—or himself?

Well, she decided before closing her eyes at long last, fooling him could be quite fun!

CHAPTER TWELVE

A LOUD thumping on the front door disturbed Rosanna's dreamless sleep. Donning a dressing-gown and only half awake, she slouched down the little hall and opened the door to Rhona.

'Hello. Sorry about the rude awakening,' Rhona said. 'I was just about to turn tail and go to Switchboard to borrow the master key. I've a lot to do, packing, seeing Stuart for that all-important reference, then there's a train to catch to Manchester Airport.'

'But it's only six in the morning!' Rosanna protested, drowsily pushing her ash-blonde hair back away from her eyes.

'Don't I know it! I came down on the milk train, or was it one carrying mail and daily newspapers as well? I don't know. I simply persuaded the guard to let me on by claiming to be a doctor attending an urgent case.' Rhona chuckled wryly. 'He didn't guess I meant a *suit*case!'

She hurried into her bedroom. 'Did you enjoy Singapore?' she called back, then without waiting for an answer continued, 'What was Song like when you saw him last? Happy? Had he grown at all? Cut a tooth yet?'

'You were with him a mere two weeks ago!' Rosanna stared after her, thinking Rhona must be even more confused than she was herself.

'It's been a long two weeks,' Rhona sighed loudly. 'He seems to grow daily, doesn't he? I'm aching to see him again, hold him in my arms, cuddle him. Oh, well, it won't be long now. Be a pal and make me a hot drink, will you?'

Likening her to a frantic whirlwind, Rosanna watched bleary-eyed as Rhona flashed between rooms, searching out her belongings.

She's far more capable of putting the kettle on at this moment than I am, she thought drowsily, wishing Rhona would let her get back to bed. Nevertheless she made tea and poured out two cups.

'It's all up to Stuart now.' Rhona swept into the kitchen to take a sip from one. 'Did you manage to win him over?'

'One never knows with Stuart,' was all Rosanna could find to say.

'Oh, I hope you didn't let me down, or you'll have defeated the whole object of the exercise.' Rhona frowned at her. 'I was depending on you, you know. Now I suppose I'll have to soften up Stuart myself. It's a great nuisance, means popping in to see him first thing to give him a chance to write the reference before he starts on his ward round. What time are you supposed to be on duty?'

'Quite soon.' Rosanna continued her effort to remain pleasant. 'But there's a boy I want to see first. He's just had a twenty-third operation on his feet. He was born with them turned back to front—do you remember him? A nice lad, name of James Dixon.'

'The name rings a bell, vaguely anyway. Why, what's happened to him?'

'Nothing bad I hope. His feet should be OK now. I want to see him before he leaves hospital, that's all. He goes this morning.'

'Then you'd better get dressed, hadn't you? I'll be just as well pleased to have the flat to myself until I'm packed.'

I'm dismissed, thought Rosanna sourly, not really liking Rhona's dictatorial tone. All the same, she took advantage of the chance offered, going into her own room to get ready to go over to the orthopaedic ward to say goodbye to the youth who had so gallantly endured great pain, severe handicaps, and so many operations.

He was ready to leave, his father having come to fetch him home before going to his office.

Kevin was there too. 'Walk tall, Sunny Jim,' he admonished James Dixon humorously, 'the operative word being *walk*! Remember, none of this cadging-lifts business now you've got two good feet! And don't limp. . .unless you want to come back and be cast as Tiny "Jim" in our Christmas panto. I promise you you'd be the target for dozens of custard pies!'

'Sounds fun!' grinned James, shaking hands all round, then, blinking hard, 'I'm going to miss you a lot,' he said, biting his lip and looking down at the floor, his voice becoming muffled.

'And how do you think we'll feel?' muttered Kevin, turning away. 'You're almost part of the furniture! Come back and see us, won't you, and don't forget about the Chinaman.'

'The Chinaman?' James looked up, mystified.

'Yes,' nodded Kevin. 'The one who was always complaining about his feet. . .until the day he met a man who hadn't any!'

Winking conspiratorially at Rosanna, he hurried off, but not before she had caught a glimpse of tears in his eyes.

Her glance following the white-coated figure fast disappearing along the corridor, she chided herself for falling for the wrong man. Why couldn't she have chosen Kevin? she asked herself, after saying goodbye to James and his father. Kevin had all the attributes she most admired, and would no doubt make a wonderful father for some lucky children, as well as an ideal husband giving lots of love and understanding to whomever he chose to be his wife.

I could be that wife, she reminded herself. He's hinted at it often enough!

Then the thought of Stuart took precedence and her heart began to work faster, especially when footsteps seemed to be gaining up on her and she sensed, without looking back, that he was behind her.

'Not so fast!' Reaching out, he caught hold of her arm. 'I want to talk to you,' he said, so she waited, although she was unable to look at him for fear he would know she had been thinking of him. 'We must go and thank Mr Armstrong for the free holiday some time. Why not tonight?' he suggested.

'Why not?' Rosanna was proud of herself for answering so glibly yet coolly, even though her heart was positively hammering away in her chest.

'Oh,' he sounded taken aback, and the realisation that he had expected to have to argue her into agreement brought out the mischief in her.

'Might as well get it over,' she said. 'Then I can have my evenings to myself again.'

'I expect Peter, or even Kevin, would have something to say about that!' he remarked drily.

'You think so?' She tried to copy the Mona Lisa's enigmatic smile.

'Don't tease,' he reprimanded. 'I'll call for you at seven—if that time proves convenient for the Armstrongs. I'll phone and ask. . .and, Rosanna,' his grip tightened on her arm, 'don't flirt with Peter. Behave yourself!'

'As if I wouldn't,' she replied perkily, her grey eyes round and innocent. 'You misjudge me, Mr Gainsborough. I don't flirt with any men, not even with those who rather wish I would.'

'You certainly don't lack confidence in your ability to attract,' he muttered, withdrawing his hand from her arm and making to walk off. 'Do you think such an amount of confidence is justified?'

'I merely go by the effect it has on others,' she declared capriciously, adding, raising her voice so that he would be sure to hear, 'even on general surgeons occasionally!'

Then, pleased with herself because she felt she had shown she was not in awe of him, she turned and wandered off in the opposite direction from the one he was taking. She had to, because although she could hope to fool him, she was unable to deceive herself and knew that telltale green flecks would be dancing once again in her eyes. . .this time because her heart was rejoicing at the knowledge that she would be with him again so soon. For a whole evening, possibly!

She even warmed to Peter a little because he was throwing Stuart and herself together by insisting on them going jointly to give a personal thank-you to his father for their holiday.

Rhona phoned her in Casualty an hour or so later. 'I have my reference!' she reported joyfully. 'Stuart said there was never any doubt but that he'd give me a good one, as he had to judge me solely on my work. No, I didn't tell him about Song and Tang, they weren't mentioned. I'll leave the telling to you. I'm afraid he won't be pleased with the part you played in the deception, but no doubt you'll square him on that point, given time.'

'Won't I be seeing you again?' Rosanna felt a sudden sense of loss. Maddening as Rhona could be at times, she knew she would miss her company.

'Sorry,' Rhona answered in a panic of preparation, 'I've a train to catch and a taxi waiting. I'll drop you a line from Singapore. Thanks for the help you gave. Cheerio, must dash!'

And without any further fuss she went out of Rosanna's life, leaving a blank space. Who would fill it? Rosanna wondered, feeling sad, but then with her usual fortitude and before the sense of loneliness could blanket around her, she forced herself to concentrate on the clinic about to begin.

To her relief the busyness of the Casualty Department provided all the therapy she needed. Everyone coming in had a claim to her full attention and received it, whether patients with minor fractures needing to have plasters removed, or more complicated cases having to be reviewed.

The sheer variety of the workload kept her actively instructing the new junior doctors, besides channelling the expertise of the clinic nurses.

Referring people to other departments including Physiotherapy took time too, as did ordering and reading X-rays. Many burns needed reviewing and re-dressing, while patients who had left the short-stay ward had to be followed up.

Clinics seldom gave her time to think about herself, or even to stop for a tea or coffee, and the clinic on this particular morning was no exception.

In fact, such was her dedication and concentration that when wanting to send a patient to the surgery ward she actually spoke over the inter-hospital phone without realising it was Stuart himself to whom she was speaking, she was so fully preoccupied with thoughts of the patient's needs.

It was only afterwards, away from the hospital, that she recalled with surprise that her heart had not reacted in its usual excited way to the sound of Stuart's voice. Maybe, she thought hopefully, she was gaining control over her feelings at long last?

However, it was lonely in the flat without Rhona to chat to. She bathed, scented herself and dressed up in a flattering tan silk knee-length model garment, a cocktail dress, she supposed one could call it, then sat at the kitchen table trying to work on the audit she was involved in, but it was difficult to get her brain to function on facts and figures when all the time she was listening for Stuart's ring on the doorbell.

A ring came at last, ten minutes before the time stated on the message he had left for her with a switchboard operator.

Pushing her papers together, Rosanna rose and walked to the door, only to find Alexa on the doorstep and looking more glamorous than ever, carefully made up, beautifully dressed.

'Hasn't Stuart arrived yet?' she queried, stepping into the hall and peering over Rosanna's shoulder. 'He told me to be ready by ten to seven, and it's that now.'

'Why, where are you going?' asked Rosanna, surprised at the turn events were taking.

'Coming with you. He wanted me to make up a foursome. . .you and Peter, he and I.'

'I thought Stuart and I were having dinner at the Armstrongs',' Rosanna mumbled, feeling confused and not a little put out.

'We all are.' Alexa dusted one of the kitchen chairs with a clean dish towel and sat down. 'Then going on to a nightclub. . .without the old man, of course. He isn't feeling too well, apparently.'

'So that's why the change of arrangements?'

'Not necessarily.' Alexa gave no further explanation, but her smug expression spoke volumes!

The evening already spoilt for her, Rosanna made no attempt to answer the door when Stuart rang a few minutes later. She gave Alexa the privilege, not that she could have stopped her taking it. She had never seen Stuart's secretary move so fast.

'Ready? Good girl, you look great,' she heard Stuart say with approval, then he glanced into the kitchen. 'Come on, Cinderella,' he said to Rosanna, and he might have meant it humorously; nevertheless she fumed inwardly, feeling belittled.

If she could have locked herself in her bedroom refusing to come out, she would have, she avowed, bitterly regretting the fact that none of the doors inside the flat had locks.

Then her sense of humour took over and she could see the funny side of what was happening. She had no recourse, she decided, but to make the best of things as they were. She only hoped the dinner would help salvage the situation, although if she was to be stuck with Peter for the evening—well, it would take more than a sense of humour to help her along!

She did have the satisfaction of seeing Alexa escorted into the back seat of the car, whereas the front seat was assigned to her, but whether that was a compliment or not, she had no idea. Perhaps Stuart looked upon her as being the more humbly staid and sedate of the two, almost elderly, in fact? She wouldn't put it past him!

Conversation was desultory, Alexa obviously aggrieved at having to sit in the back of the car, Stuart concentrating on driving, and Rosanna rather mischievously enjoying Alexa's discomfiture.

The night was chilly, clouds covered the moon and there was little to see except the occasional shadowy outline of a house, tree or farm building. Ghostly cows broke the atmosphere with a moo now and then, a dog barked in the distance and sheep bleated when an owl hooted, otherwise there was nothing to break the silence other than the sound of the car engine.

'Not as romantic as Singapore, is it?' Rosanna said out loud, hoping Alexa could hear. 'But of course there was bright moonlight there, palm trees to wander under, lanterns of every shape and colour. . . remember the Tunnel of Love, Stuart?'

He returned a blank stare.

'Oh, don't be so bashful!' Rosanna taunted, thoroughly enjoying herself in the role she was trying to play. 'Don't you think he's one of the world's foremost romantics?' She threw the question back over her shoulder to Alexa, who, however, made no response, pretending to be asleep when Rosanna looked towards her for an answer.

'This must be the Armstrongs' place—according to the directions I was given.' Still distancing himself from the unfriendly atmosphere inside the car, Stuart drove in through large wide-open ornamental gates. 'Quite an imposing mansion,' he remarked.

Alexa needed no awakening. She was instantly alert enough to gather her designer-styled wrap around her, ready to step out of the car when it stopped before the wide steps leading up to a huge studded oak door which at that very moment was being thrown open by a butler.

Peter appeared welcomingly in the doorway and, taking Rosanna's arm, led the way into a large baronial hall which had a minstrels' gallery running around it.

Mr Armstrong came forward to shake hands with the guests, a maid following behind ready to take the girls' wraps and show the way to a luxurious powder-room.

Alexa was very impressed. She showed it in her eyes and in the way she bore herself, walking proudly almost as if she owned the place.

The dinner was beautifully served, and delicious in every way, and afterwards the Armstrongs and their guests adjourned to a comfortable lounge to relax by a great log fire.

'This is the life,' Stuart's attitude seemed to say, as with his long legs stretched out before him he relaxed into a wide leather armchair.

Leaving her own chair, Alexa sat on the arm of his, Peter watching and not looking too happy about it.

Having duly thanked Mr Armstrong for the expenses-paid holiday, Stuart and Rosanna between them gave him a résumé of the things they had seen, and much of what they had done in Singapore, and the conversation became quite lively.

However, it was soon apparent that Peter was getting bored. Alexa was not too happy either. 'Come,' he said to her, drawing her away from Stuart's chair, 'I'll show you around. You'll appreciate some of our collector's items and treasures, I'm sure. Dad's gathered them from the four corners of the earth!'

'How marvellous!' gushed Alexa. 'I'd love to travel and see exotic places!' And, brightening up, she followed in his wake.

'You two come up to my room,' suggested Mr Armstrong to Stuart and Rosanna. 'I keep the best of my souvenirs up there.' And levering himself out of his chair, he walked towards the beautiful wide staircase.

Rosanna worried a little, considering him too unsteady for his own good. He was a big man, obviously overweight, had eaten a large meal, following it with brandy and a cigar, and now he was labouring up the stairs, hurrying, although obviously growing increasingly breathless with every step he took.

She looked meaningly at Stuart, to see concern reflected in his eyes too, and sure enough, no sooner had Mr Armstrong led the way into his luxurious bedroom than he more or less collapsed on to a chair.

'I get angina,' he gasped, pointing to a sublingual nitrate spray resting on his dressing-table.

Quickly Rosanna passed it to him.

'Where's the pain?' asked Stuart, bending over him.

'Middle of chest, feels like an elephant sitting on me!' Mr Armstrong slumped down to the floor.

'Pain radiates to left arm?' Rosanna suggested.

The big man nodded as best he could. Then, 'I feel sick,' he mumbled.

'Very sweaty and pale,' whispered Rosanna to Stuart. 'I'm calling an ambulance!'

Stuart nodded. 'Tell them myocardial infarction.'

'Of course.' She ran to the bedside phone while Stuart sat Mr Armstrong up in his position on the floor, making sure his back was supported. Almost instantly, however, he made a gasp-type sound and fell unconscious.

'It's a cardiac arrest!' Rosanna and Stuart exclaimed as one, immediately applying external cardiac massage and mouth-to-mouth resuscitation.

The ambulance arrived, the crew bringing up equipment and taking over the cardiac massage. Rosanna immediately inserted an intravenous cannula, the second ambulance man attached Mr Armstrong to a cardiac monitor while Stuart inserted an airway and started ventilating by ambu-bag.

'Monitor shows asystoli—can I have some atropine, please!' Rosanna called urgently to the men, then, after waiting two minutes after giving the atropine, 'He's still in asystoli,' she said, 'so I'll try adrenalin this time.'

'Good,' Stuart said approvingly, looking at the monitor. 'He's now in ventricular fibrillation, so he can be electro-cardioverted.'

Immediately the ambulance crew placed the pads on Mr Armstrong's chest while Rosanna charged the electric plates, then placed them on the pads, and after checking that no one was touching Mr Armstrong, delivered the electric shock.

A few seconds later the monitor showed that his heart was beating normally at last, and he started breathing again, regaining consciousness.

'What's happened?' he asked.

'We've had to do a bit of work on your heart,' Stuart told him. 'Are you having any pain now?'

'Yes. And breathing's difficult.'

'I'll sit you up again,' said Stuart, making the effort, while Rosanna got the ambulance men to provide some diuretic, analgesic and anti-emetic drugs for her to inject.

'One's for the pain, one's to help your breathing and this last one's to stop you feeling sick,' she said as she injected the drugs through the intravenous cannula.

'I'll find Peter and let him know what's happening,' Stuart said quietly to Rosanna. 'Meet you down at the ambulance, OK?'

'Right,' Rosanna sighed wearily. 'Ask him to see Alexa back to her accommodation, will you?'

Stuart nodded. 'You'll come with me in the ambulance? We'll collect my car tomorrow.'

Rosanna was much too exhausted to do anything but nod, although the fact that he had said 'we' and not simply 'I' gave her quite a lift.

She accompanied the ambulance men as with quite a degree of difficulty they carried Mr Armstrong downstairs. Peter, his expression tense, was waiting by the ambulance, Alexa clinging to his arm.

'We owe you another great debt.' Peter's worried glance took in both Rosanna and Stuart. 'I've known for ages that my father was taking on too many business responsibilities himself. I've begged him to delegate some of them to me, to let me share the work involved, but no,' he grumbled on with some bitterness, 'he wouldn't listen, simply wouldn't listen. He'd have given me the earth, wanting me to enjoy playing with it, saying his happiness lay in providing me with the things he'd never been able to have in his own youth, but all I really wanted was the one thing he wouldn't let me have.' Peter's voice broke. 'Now perhaps he will, only please God it isn't too late.'

Stuart simply clamped a hand on his shoulder in a sympathetic gesture. 'Believe it isn't, keep trusting and giving thanks,' he said encouragingly, 'and he'll be fine.

Now if you'd see Alexa back to her home, we'll be on our way.'

'I'll be at the hospital almost as soon as you,' Peter promised as Stuart followed Rosanna into the ambulance.

'So the nightclub visit is off, is it?' they overheard Alexa saying, adding a disgruntled, 'Seems we dressed up for nothing!' at which Peter stared back at her, aghast.

'It's strange the different ways in which people react to shock,' was all Stuart commented, and Rosanna sighed, sure he was making excuses for Alexa again.

Then she also recalled him saying, *'We'll* collect the car tomorrow,' and how she had thrilled, thinking he intended to take her with him, whereas probably he had meant Alexa all the time!

Guiltily putting such thoughts aside, feeling them unworthy at such a stressful time for the Armstrongs, Rosanna concentrated on doing all she could to cheer Peter up when he arrived at his father's bedside.

Claiming exhaustion, Alexa had retired to her own flat.

Finally as Mr Armstrong's condition seemed stable, Stuart and Rosanna left the coronary care unit, both having early morning ward rounds to consider.

'I'm glad we were there to help,' Stuart spoke heavily as they parted outside Rosanna's flat. 'Thanks for all you did.' He tried to hide a yawn.

'Thanks to you too,' murmured Rosanna, sleepily fishing in her evening bag for her door key.

'Got it?' asked Stuart. 'Well, goodnight then, or should I say good morning?' And, reaching for her, he drew her close, then kissed her full on the lips.

'I needed that tonic,' he said. 'Now perchance to dream!'

Rosanna was too astounded to say anything. Even when she was in bed she found it hard to believe the kiss had really happened. It must be his own particular reaction to shock, she assured herself—and, too tired to bother analysing his feelings further, smiled as she fell asleep.

CHAPTER THIRTEEN

PETER remained in the hospital all night. Rosanna saw him in passing when she went to do a ward round of the short-stay ward first thing in the morning.

'How *is* your father?' she asked.

'Doing surprisingly well, they tell me,' Peter replied with a wan smile. 'But it was a close thing, wasn't it? I've never been more scared in my life! Sorry if I went on about him last night—I can't believe now that I actually grumbled about him, but I know I did.'

'Shock reaction, that's what it was,' said Rosanna, remembering Stuart's words.'We all know you're very fond of him really.'

'He's great!' Peter's eyes filled.

'Have you had any breakfast?' she asked, concerned for him because he looked so emotionally strained and pale.

'Not yet.'

'Then come along with me for another look at your dad, then I'll get one of the nurses to take you down to the canteen during her break. You must get something to eat—there's no sense in you neglecting your food and making yourself ill again. Your father's going to need you as never before, so whatever you do, you must keep up your own strength.'

'I suppose you're right.' Peter walked along with her to the coronary care unit. His father was still asleep, however, so Rosanna sent him along to the canteen in the company of the lively young student nurse, Sue, who was about to go there herself.

Sue, who could have her pick of the hospital's eligible young men, seemingly inspiring most of them with the wish to marry her, yet finding her not all that easy to catch. She, thought Rosanna, would be able to handle Peter all right, and would be a much better choice for him than Alexa. . .or herself!

'That was a foolhardy gesture on your part,' Stuart remarked, happening to come along the corridor at that moment. 'Haven't you ever heard the old adage, "Never introduce your donor to a pal"?'

Rosanna bristled. 'Why, what do you mean?' she asked, although she knew perfectly well what he meant.

'Pairing Peter off with a pretty nurse when he's at his most vulnerable?'

She merely shrugged. 'I must go, I've got work to do.' And she walked on.

'Coming out this evening?' he asked, catching up with her.

'Isn't it Alexa's turn?' she asked coldly, then felt furious with herself for mentioning the one person she wanted him to forget!

'Be ready at eight,' was all he said before hurrying towards some stairs and taking them three at a time, leaving Rosanna to just stand and stare after him.

The nerve of him. . .taking it for granted I'll be at his beck and call! she muttered to herself, resentment building up again. Soon, however, she had too many problems to sort out in Casualty to be able to give time to untangling her own mixed feelings.

At eight in the evening, deliberately deserting her flat, not wanting to be there when Stuart called, she visited the coronary care unit again. Peter was there still, sitting by his father's bed.

'I'll never be able to thank you and Stuart enough for what you did for Dad,' he said quietly, his eyes unusually earnest.

'We only did what we've been trained to do,'

Rosanna answered. 'Are you staying here tonight again?'

He nodded.

'Then make sure you have some decent food sent up from the canteen,' she suggested.

'Sue's arranging that for me,' he replied.

'Oh, good.' Feeling relieved of responsibility towards him, Rosanna could find no other excuse to remain in the hospital, so, not knowing where else to go, she went back to her flat.

A taxi was waiting outside it. Stuart jumped out, drew the white coat she was carrying away from her arm and threw it on to the back seat, ushering her in to sit beside it.

'You're coming as you are,' he insisted. 'We'll collect your wrap from the Armstrongs' house. You left it there last night when you came here with me in the ambulance, remember?'

'Of course. And you left your car behind.'

'Which explains why the taxi.' His lips curled a little derisively, she thought, although it could have been amusement on his part, one never knew with Stuart. . .so, not being too sure of the mood he was in, she moved along the seat to sit as far from him as possible, but to her surprise as soon as he sat down his arm went out to encircle her and draw her nearer.

'No seat-belts here in the back,' he pointed out, 'so I must protect you myself to keep you safe. Besides, I feel lost without having the driving to do!'

The taxi-driver started up the engine and, under cover of the noise it made, Stuart murmured, 'That kiss last night fired me with a longing for more,' tipping Rosanna's face up towards his, then without waiting for permission he kissed her again, this time with even more fervour.

'I'm beginning to positively yearn for you, Rosanna,' he whispered. 'You distract me even in my work. I don't know how I compare with Peter in your eyes, but you can't expect me to simply sit back and let him steal you from me.'

The warmth of his arm was comforting, his kiss exciting. Rosanna gave up all attempt to pretend she was unwilling to have him kiss her yet again, finding it difficult enough not to return kiss for kiss, managing to desist only by concentrating her mind on Alexa.

For, as she reminded herself, she had as little wish to be compared with Alexa as Stuart had to be compared with Peter. So as soon as they had transferrred to Stuart's Mercedes convertible after retrieving her wrap from the Armstrong home, she suggested they should have a meal somewhere, claiming to be both tired and hungry—although in truth she was thinking more along the lines of finding safety in numbers, suddenly feeling shy of remaining alone with Stuart in the romantic mood he was in.

'Of course,' he answered her suggestion solicitously. 'We'll stop for food at the first hotel we come to.'

When they left after dining, the world around them was silvered with moonshine and very beautiful, stars shining in a clear sky.

'A dark blue sky,' Stuart remarked, looking up at it. Then peering down at her, he murmured, 'As mysteriously dark as your grey eyes when they're angry. I used to think your eyes matched the faded blue of theatre gowns, then I found they were grey. . .your eyes, I mean, not the gowns.'

Rosanna smiled, amused in spite of herself.

'You haven't said much.' Stuart took hold of her hand before starting up the car again. 'Is it just a case of exhaustion, or are you wishing you were with someone else?'

'Oh no!' She simply could not allow him to think he was a disappointment.

He leaned over from the driving seat, his face close,

his breath warm, his lips near. She put up a hand to ward him off, but he caught it in his, kissing each finger in turn. Then because while she looked at him her lips had parted, he covered them with his own in a tender, loving kiss.

Love was all around. Their world was full of it, the moon beaming, stars shining, banks of honeysuckle delicately perfuming the air.

'I think I'm falling in love,' Stuart whispered, gently smoothing Rosanna's hair back from her forehead before placing butterfly-light kisses on her eyelids, her ears, and, light-heartedly, on the very tip of her short slightly tiptilted nose.

She laughed with him, not at him. The whole universe seemed to pivot on a shaft of sheer, glorious happiness. It was a magical, mystical few moments, and Rosanna was enraptured. 'I love you,' she longed to cry out from her heart, but the fear of being rebuffed was so strong that it held the words back.

She was not sure enough of him, that was the trouble, she told herself, not realising that doubts once entertained quickly became convictions. Why had he asked whether she'd prefer to be with someone else? Was it because he himself wished he had a different companion. . . Alexa, for instance?

'I think you'd better take me back to my flat,' she murmured, suddenly indescribably weary. 'I'm very tired, Stuart, and I think you're taking unfair advantage of that fact.'

Immediately the words were out she regretted them.

'You don't care for me, is that what you're trying to say?' Taking umbrage, abruptly he released her from his hold. 'Then why do you tempt me so?' he growled. 'Leading me up to the heights, then unfeelingly dropping me right down to the depths!'

'You're tired too.' Aghast at herself, she tried to provide him with an excuse, realising she had made him feel rejected. 'Please take me home, otherwise we'll only end up wounding each other with words we don't mean,' she said sadly. 'Last night was very stressful for us both. We need to sleep it off.'

He drove straight back to the hospital, where, apart from going round to her side of the car and opening her door, he virtually ignored her, saying nothing except a curt, 'Goodnight'. Then, after waiting to see her go indoors, he drove off.

Refusing to allow herself to ponder over the evening's events for fear of losing more sleep and feeling worse than ever the next day, Rosanna concentrated on getting to bed as quickly as she could.

She was greeted by Sister Mills when she arrived in Casualty in the morning. 'Watch your step with Mr Jackson in the end bed there,' Sister warned her. 'Although he's in his eighties he's as chirpy as a young bird, flirts with every female in sight, but don't worry, he's nice with it as long as you give as good as you get. He respects that.'

'Why has he come in?' Rosanna was immediately all doctor again, the patients her main concern.

'Fell when he was up a ladder lopping a branch off a tree. . .should have had more sense at his age!' Sister Mills clucked her tongue disapprovingly, nevertheless, 'Coming, Mr Jackson!' she replied promptly when he beckoned to her and, all smiles, she went straight over to him.

'I simply can't resist that saucy look in his eye,' she declared in an aside to Rosanna as she passed her.

The inter-hospital phone rang just then and, a nurse not being available at that moment, Rosanna answered it.

'Is that you, Rosanna?' Stuart asked down the line. 'Well, I've got to see you. We need to talk.'

Wondering why the urgency, she suggested he should

come round to her flat after they had finished their work for the day.

He sounded as if he would find the waiting hard, so when he hadn't turned up by seven o'clock after working since eight that morning Rosanna worried, knowing that he, like herself, should really have been free since five.

She had a meal prepared, a table set. Eight o'clock struck, then nine, but still he failed to arrive.

Finally he came. It was ten o'clock. His face was haggard and drawn.

'It's my niece,' he burst out immediately she opened the front door to him. 'She's developed meningitis. I've just come back from seeing her in a London hospital. I could have done with your company and support, Rosanna. She's very poorly.' He blinked hard and fast. 'This is a blow my brother could well have done without. I phoned my grandfather in New Zealand, and he gave me another shock—said he's getting married again.'

His expression grew more strained. 'Not that I mind Grandad remarrying, don't get me wrong. I'll be glad to know he isn't on his own any more, he's been very lonely since Grandma died. But the thing is, he was going to have the girls over to his New Zealand home for their school holidays. *Now* what can I do with them? If Sheila recovers, and please God she will, she'll need careful looking after for a time. Oh, everything's a terrible mess!'

He sat looking so desolate that Rosanna moved to put a sympathetic arm about his shoulders. He caught at her hand and rested his cheek against it. 'She's very poorly, Rosanna. It will just about kill my brother if he has to lose her as well as losing his wife!'

'Stop looking on the black side!' Rosanna spoke quite severely. 'You're meeting anguish halfway. Perhaps none of the things you fear will happen.'

She would have liked to remind him of the antagon-
ism dividing them the previous evening only to disappear without trace already, but to remind him of
anything so disrupting would seem cruel, although it
might illustrate her point about worrying in vain.

Instead she asked, 'Are you quite sure your niece
has meningitis?'

'All the symptoms are there; vomiting, headaches,
stiff neck, rashes. . .'

'And what treatment is she getting?'

'She's had a lumbar puncture—all the usual things.'

'Who first diagnosed meningitis?' she asked.

'The school's GP. The Mother Superior called him
in, and immediately he gave Sheila an injection of
antibiotic and sent her into hospital.'

'And?' Rosanna prompted.

'Well, she collapsed when she arrived, became semi-
conscious, so the paediatrics took her over, placed her
into Intensive Care where they're continuing the antibiotic treatment.'

It was only with difficulty that Rosanna could distinguish his words, he was mumbling so, sitting at the
kitchen table, head now in hands, obviously deeply
upset.

'It's a blessing the GP started her on antibiotics so
early,' Rosanna remarked,trying to cheer him up.
'Well, look, you can't do anything more than pray for
her tonight. There's a seven o'clock Mass in the
hospital chapel tomorrow morning—let's make a
special effort to get to that, then I'll drive down with
you to see Sheila.'

'You will? You mean it?' Stuart brightened.

'That's if you'd like me to, of course. I'll have to get
someone to cover my duties, but that shouldn't present
any great problem. I've still a couple of days' holiday
owing to me, I'll take that.'

'Unless,' she hesitated, but simply could not resist

adding, 'unless you'd prefer Alexa to accompany you instead?'

He looked up then, the answer in his eyes.

In an effort not to blush, and to cover feelings of guilt and shame because she had again allowed jealousy to personalise the conversation, Rosanna became very down to earth.

'Now, can I make you a hot drink and a sandwich?' she asked, busying herself at the kitchen sink and taking care not to allow herself to mention that the meal she had prepared so much earlier was irredeemably ruined.

Stuart shook his head to all offers of food and drink, however. 'No, thanks, I'll get to bed. I'm very tired, and you must be too,' he said.

Then, standing up, placing anxiety-trembling hands on her shoulders and turning her round to face him, he held her close for a second or two before kissing her gently on her forehead, and, all his customary signs of arrogance disappearing, said, 'You're very sweet and forgiving, and I don't deserve it after the way I treated you last night, but. . .thank you. . .' Then he left.

He was already in the little chapel when Rosanna went there in the morning, and almost all through Mass he remained on his knees, head bowed, but when about to go to the altar to receive Holy Communion he reached out towards her and pressed her hand appreciatively, making a bond between them which once again filled her heart with love and hope.

After a snack breakfast in a motorway service station on the way down to London they arrived at the hospital to find Sheila making good progress, and a fax awaiting Stuart from his grandfather and sent care of the hospital.

'He's coming over!' Stuart exclaimed, reading it. 'Wants to get married over here with me as best man! Imagine that!' The thought tickled his sense of humour.

'Best man to one's grandfather—whatever next!' he actually grinned. Then, going back to the fax sheet, 'He says he'll be taking the girls back to New Zealand with him.' Stuart continued. 'Apparently he's already bought a house near where my brother's receiving treatment, his aim being to keep the girls in touch with their father. He's a wonderful man, isn't he, I told you he was, but I didn't expect him to beat me in the marriage stakes. Here, read this for yourself.' He handed it over to Rosanna.

Feeling privileged, she read it more thoroughly than he had. 'Your future stepgrandmother sounds nice,' she said. 'Especially in the way she's welcoming the girls. She's a good few years younger than your grandfather, by the sound of it, so maybe she'll be able to cope.'

'She'll need to.' The anxiety lines on Stuart's face smoothed out a little more as a sense of relief took over. 'Those nieces of mine can be quite a handful when they're feeling fit, which, please God, they will be from now on, because it does look as if Sheila will make a good recovery; the meningitis must have been caught in time.'

'And you're happy once more.' Rosanna's eyes glowed with warmth and satisfaction. 'I *told* you not to meet anguish halfway, didn't I! See, your fears came to nothing.' Her deep sigh was one of relief and thanksgiving. 'So how long do you intend staying in London?' she asked.

'Well, since you have only the two free days, I'll drive you back to our hospital tomorrow, then come down here to stay with Sheila until Grandad arrives, which should be within a further three days. If all continues to go well with Sheila, the family will probably all come up to stay in a hotel near us to finalise the wedding plans, then when the celebrations are over, I suppose they'll be off to New Zealand. . .all four of them together.'

'So it's not likely they'll stay here for Christmas? That's a pity. They could have seen the medics panto!'

'I wouldn't want to put them through that trauma!' Stuart grimaced humorously. The change in him was remarkable, Rosanna was thinking, eyeing him shrewdly. He seemed to have cast his worries to the wind, the improvement in Sheila's condition making all the difference. Or was it that her illness had made him come to grips with the things that really mattered in life?

'Why, don't you think they'd enjoy the medics' panto?' she asked, just to see what he would say.

'I fear Grandfather's lady would be shocked by it,' Stuart replied seriously. 'Not many people understand that in our walk of life it's necessary sometimes to let rip and make light of the sometimes terrible things we have to see and do.'

'But you wouldn't be worried about your grandad's reaction?' asked Rosanna.

'Yes, I would,' he grinned broadly for the first time. 'Knowing him, he'd probably die laughing!'

'And the girls?'

'Oh, they'd be all right, they wouldn't know what anyone was talking about, all the double meanings in medical jargon would pass straight over their heads, as I imagine they did when you were doing surgery and working in Theatre? You didn't seem to get *your* sense of humour tainted, I've noticed.'

'I ignored what I didn't want to hear, realising it was necessary for some surgeons to let off steam or they wouldn't have been able to carry on. It's a pretty brutal profession when one thinks of it. Brutal, but someone has to do it or many people would be left to suffer unnecessarily.'

'Profound thinking,' Stuart commented. 'Now, what about some lunch?'

The rest of the day was spent in or around the hospital, frequently keeping an eye on Sheila's condition, which fortunately remained stable, then even began to improve, leaving Stuart and Rosanna in each other's company for many long hours.

It had been a time for really getting to know one another, Rosanna thought with some satisfaction as she lay in her bed in a nearby hotel, and she went to sleep longing for the morning to come and wondering what the day would bring.

CHAPTER FOURTEEN

THE next day started well, Sheila having regained consciousness, being so much better in fact that she had been moved from Intensive Care to the main ward.

Rosanna and Stuart set off on their long drive in cheerful mood, chatting inconsequentially about this and that, then suddenly Stuart changed, becoming much more serious. 'Do you miss your friend, Dr Morris?' he asked out of the blue.

Rosanna looked at him, surprised at the question. 'Of course,' she said, wondering what was in his mind.

He raised an eyebrow and cast a quick frown in her direction. 'I suppose she's been reunited with Song and Tang by now,' he queried more than stated.

Rosanna was unsure about what to say in return, then decided it was time she told him the truth. 'I heard you gave her a good reference,' she began, adding a tentative and rather nervous, 'But did you know *before* that Song. . .'

'Was *her* child?' he butted in. 'Yes. When you left Singapore so abruptly I went along to the hospital. Young Song was no longer there. However, I was put in touch with his father, Tang.' He glanced sideways at Rosanna. 'He was far more communicative than you—told me the whole story.'

'He had the right to do so,' she muttered defensively. 'I hadn't. I'd promised not to.'

'He told me that too.'

'So you knew about the deception? You didn't say anything to me about it. . .'

'There were other things on my mind, matters which filled my heart,' he told her.

'But you didn't know about Sheila's illness then.' Rosanna blushed, knowing what she wanted him to say and trying to edge him into saying it. 'Something else must have been distracting you?' She looked away to the passing landscape, awaiting his reply.

'I didn't know about a lot of things,' Stuart remarked drily. 'About the pain of loving someone who loved someone else, for instance.'

Which was not what Rosanna was expecting to hear. Her head turned back towards him. 'I don't know what you mean.' There was a sad note of pleading in her voice. She too was about to be hurt again, she knew it, nevertheless, 'Please tell me,' she prompted.

'I think you know very well. I wasn't so worried about Kevin Berry, being well aware that he enjoys flirting with one girl after another, not being ready to settle down yet, but when Peter Armstrong came on the scene you changed.'

'You're *jealous*!' Rosanna exclaimed, relieved. 'Just as jealous as I was over Alexa when I saw you'd sent her a postcard from Singapore!'

'I did no such thing! I sent one to the department as a whole. It's the normal custom, especially when one visits far-off countries one's staff might not have seen.'

'And she said you'd asked to take her out to dinner when you returned.'

'Oh, was that what bothered you?' he laughed. 'Actually she did ask me to escort her to some function or other, but I made an excuse not to. Accompanying Sister Mills would be more to my liking. She might be twice my age, but at least *she* shows some spirit.'

Without looking towards Rosanna he added, 'I like a girl to have spirit, even if it's a fiery one such as you have at times!'

Rosanna smiled then. 'Haven't we been silly?' she sighed. 'Each at loggerheads with the other so often, and for such nonsensical reasons. How can there ever be peace in the world when even two people with similar aims, like us, can't agree?'

'We've been behaving like children.' Stuart nodded in agreement, touching her hand and pressing her fingers tenderly before releasing them. 'Look, shall we make an effort to act as mature adults and call a permanent truce, then pop in to Manchester's Chinatown—we're near there now—to sample the mooncakes we never got around to buying in Singapore? I'm told they have some here with delicious butter pastry and macadamia nuts. I'd like to try those. You can have any sort you fancy,' he added generously. 'I feel like giving you the world, Rosanna, let alone the moon, so Chinatown, here we come!'

'They don't have a tunnel of love there, do they?' Rosanna asked a little timidly, wondering how to cope with the new light-hearted Stuart.

'We won't need one,' he asserted with a return to his more usual air of superiority, causing a thrill to shiver down Rosanna's backbone. At least, that was how she described the feeling to herself.

She eyed him warily, wondering whether she dared ask the question she longed to ask, then, throwing caution to the wind, decided to risk it.

'I've often wondered. . .' she began rather shyly, afterwards pouring out the rest of her words in an embarrassed rush '. . .what you thought that morning in Singapore when Peter strove to make it appear I'd spent the night in his room?'

'I was annoyed because you'd allowed yourself to be inveigled into such a compromising situation, but it would take more than a jealous man to convince me you'd acted improperly in any way. I think I'm a better judge of character than that.'

'Thank you,' Rosanna said simply.

'Does my answer warrant a kiss?'

'Not here, not now. Keep your eyes on the road!'

'No need,' Stuart said vibrantly. 'I'm parking.' Brazenly he stole the kiss he wanted as soon as they left the car and before they made their way to Chinatown.

Shortly afterwards, holding hands and each carrying a bag of mooncakes, savoury flavoured ones for Stuart, plainer for Rosanna, they returned to the car park.

'I didn't have to do any haggling,' Rosanna boasted.

'No. Mooncakes come easier than kisses,' Stuart sighed. 'When do I get another—now?' He drew her towards him.

'No. I ration them,' Rosanna demurred. 'Besides, there are too many people around.'

'Very well, we'll go somewhere quieter.' He handed her back into the car and instead of driving straight back to her flat made a wide detour and parked on a little-known road crossing the high moorland skirting the Whiddop reservoir. 'I love the ruggedness of this region,' he said softly. 'The views, spaciousness, even the sense of brooding sadness lift me right out of this world.' Gently he pulled Rosanna closer.

'Why people want to live in towns beats me,' he continued, his cheek nestling in the silkiness of her hair. 'Just look around and see the fast-flowing Pennine streams, silver threads among the golden fronds of dying ferns serving to enhance the tweedy look of distant hills. Here even the loneliness has something special to offer.'

He sighed. 'Do you feel as I feel?' he asked. 'At one with nature, immersed in the beauty and wonder of creation? Your heart uplifted by the song of birds, delighting in the sight of so many heathers. . .each tiny bloom on every sprig perfectly shaped, bell-like or rounded, no two exactly alike?'

Rosanna rested back against his shoulder. 'It's a wonderful world,' she agreed dreamily. 'I don't know how anyone could think that everything just "happened" when it's so obviously been well thought out, the result of meticulous planning, every single thing brilliantly catered for, and individually designed, no two things ever exactly alike, whether the tallest trees or the tiniest babies, or even simple blades of grass. . .besides, how could love, or instinct, or any of our feelings have manufactured themselves?'

'Often when I'm doing surgery I marvel at the incredible organisation involved in the human body, everything packed in so beautifully,' Stuart said, starting up the car again. 'But don't let me talk shop or I'll never get back to little Sheila. I mustn't forget her.'

Driving on, they disturbed clouds of rooks as the car neared the Haworth Parsonage where the famous Brontë sisters once lived.

'It's a museum now, isn't it?' Rosanna remarked when they stopped to look at it and wander a little way along the two-mile Enfield Side walk the sisters had favoured so much. 'And I think I once read that here's where Charlotte Brontë caught the cold that led to her early death. If she was out looking for their famous waterfall she probably walked miles—look, it's only a mere trickle over moss-covered rocks!'

'Don't rob it of its romantic connotations.' Stuart put an arm about her waist. 'Look, there's no one else here, so can I have my kiss now? I've been very patient.'

There seemed no reason to refuse. Rosanna raised her face to his, and looking around afterwards knew she would remember the day, the place and the kiss for ever, for it was as if a ray of sunshine had completely dispelled the air of sadness Stuart had remarked on earlier, leaving behind only the glorious thrill of a happiness such as she had never known before.

'On we must go,' Stuart broke the spell, smiling with unaccustomed tenderness and leading her back to the car. 'But how on earth am I going to force myself to leave you when we get to the hospital? That's what bothers me.'

And how can I let you go? Rosanna wanted to ask, but a new diffidence prevented her. Love, she was thinking, was so precious, yet so fragile that just one wrong word could carry it away, perhaps never to return.

So she stayed very quiet, leaving Stuart to do the talking—something he seemed happy enough to do, educating her about the moors' lime-free water being so essential for the successful washing, carding and combing of wool which, as he informed her at length, had resulted in forests of mill chimneys springing up in the valleys, and sheep being pastured everywhere to supply the necessary wool.

Unable to match his enthusiasm for the history of the moors, Rosanna eventually lost the battle against an overwhelming drowsiness and fell asleep.

When she awakened she was outside her flat.

'Sorry if I bored you,' Stuart said bluntly.

'Oh, no, I was very interested,' she protested, then, seeing the scepticism in his eyes, she knew she had indeed said the wrong thing. Several words wrong. . .when all it took was just one careless word to send love flying away!

Saying he had better get back to Sheila, refusing to come in and wait for a meal, Stuart left quite suddenly, taking with him the loving feeling which had imbued the very air between them for so many miles before.

Rosanna was desolate. Stopping only for a quick sandwich and cup of coffee in the canteen, she returned to the accident ward looking for distraction, although she was not really due there until the next morning.

Immediately she found herself in the middle of a furore. A patient had been brought back from X-Ray and put in a bed in the accident ward instead of being taken back to the medical ward. He was looking worried, shaking a puzzled head even over the meal set out on the tray before him.

Then a porter brought in another man, halting the trolley by the occupied bed. 'Who's been sleeping in *my* bed?' the second patient asked with a dry humour. '*I* was in it until I went down to X-Ray!'

'And *I* should be in the medical ward, so what am I doing here?' asked the first man. 'This isn't even the dinner I ordered!'

Seeing Rosanna, the porter turned to her, scratching his head. 'They're so alike,' he explained apologetically, 'both in their fifties, balding, lean. . .'

By the time she had things sorted out everyone was seeing the funny side, the patients, nursing staff and Rosanna herself all enjoying a good laugh over the unintentional muddle.

She next turned her attention to pacifying a child who wanted to leave without waiting to see a doctor.

'Why?' Rosanna asked.

''Cause Mummy said, "Be quiet for five minutes and I'll let you buy a carrot for when you make a snowman." Well, I've been quiet, so now I want to go and get the carrot.'

'For a snowman? I think you'd better wait until it snows,' said Rosanna, looking out of the window towards a cloudless if frosty sky and almost wishing for a blizzard if only to satisfy the child.

He gave in, to be seen by a doctor meanwhile, however, so she was able to help clear the rest of the cards and leave the department in order to attend a scheduled X-ray meeting.

Kevin was there, friendly and lively as usual. 'Where's Stuart?' he asked when the X-ray meeting was over.

'In London. His niece is in hospital there.'

'You went down with him?'

She nodded, not really wanting to talk about Stuart.

'And you've come back worn out. There's only one thing to do. Come out with me this evening, paint the town red!'

She smiled. Kevin normally had that effect on her, helping to chase the blues away. And by nine o'clock they were enjoying a dinner and dance in his golf clubhouse.

At least, Rosanna was trying to enjoy it, knowing she should, but the thought of Stuart tended to cast a shadow over the evening.

She felt mean, unable to rival Kevin's gaiety, so he saw her back to her flat long before midnight.

'It's no good, Rosanna, is it?' he said, having a glass of wine with her in the little lounge. 'Your mind is preoccupied, caught up with Stuart. You'd marry him if you could, wouldn't you?'

She studied her glass, blinking hard to keep tears at bay.

'You're a much nicer person than he is,' she murmured, then looking up with a wistful smile tried to add a mischievous, 'Why can't I marry *you*?'

'Don't torment me.' Kevin became serious for a moment. 'For one thing, I haven't asked you, for another it isn't Leap Year, and finally, conclusively, I wouldn't want a wife whose heart belonged to someone else!'

'Well then, I'll have to stay single for the rest of my life,' she said, unsuccessfully trying to continue in a humorous vein when all she was really wanting was to have a bit of a cry, and not because of what Kevin had said, but because she was realising that she had indeed given her heart to Stuart, the very unpredictable Stuart.

'What can I do?' she asked miserably. 'I seem to be making an awful mess of things—we're forever fighting!'

'I'll tell you what to do. Stop hitting back at him,

look for his good points, encourage him a little. . .get in before Alexa snatches him away.'

'You think she could?' Rosanna stared, horrified.

'Are you prepared to risk it?' Kevin asked. 'One never knows how anyone will act on the rebound, so it's up to you, my love.' He stood up. 'Now wise old Uncle Kevin must take his leave and give you a chance to digest his words of wisdom. They might well be the only ones he'll ever utter, so cherish them!'

Bending, he gave her a gentle peck on the cheek, then, walking into the little hallway, he let himself out.

Two days later Stuart returned from London, and that evening, after completing the operations he had listed for the day, he presented himself at Rosanna's front door.

'I hope you received my message?' he asked shortly, remaining standing stiffly upright on the doorstep, his hands behind his back 'That Sheila's so much better she'll be able to leave hospital this coming weekend?'

'Yes, and she was delighted with the bouquet you sent.'

'Alexa passed on the message.' We're talking like strangers, thought Rosanna, saddening—also mentally biting her tongue for mentioning Alexa again.

'I'm glad to hear that,' Stuart said drily. 'I thought she might forget, as she's on the point of leaving.'

'Alexa, leaving?' She looked at him, startled. Was he going to give her more shocks? Announce that he and Alexa were getting married, perhaps? 'Please come in,' she pleaded, needing to sit down herself.

'Just for a moment, then,' he said. 'I only really called to give you these. . .' Bringing a hand round from behind his back, he produced two dozen red roses beautifully wrapped and ribboned. 'A peace-offering,' he said, allowing humour to crinkle his deep-set eyes. 'From me, not from Peter this time.'

'They're lovely! Thank you.' Rosanna was by now quite convinced that she had indeed lost out to Alexa, just as Kevin had warned her she might.

She busied herself opening the kitchen cupboards under the pretext of seeking a vase for the roses. Furiously blinking tears away, she could not bring herself to look towards Stuart, the man she had lost, the only man she had ever wanted.

'I think I gave Alexa a fair trial as secretary,' he was saying reflectively, standing by the table. 'But even after six months' probation she was no better than at the start. She's obviously not cut out for office work. . .so I had to do a re-think. Admin's advertising the secretarial vacancy.'

'And you're going to *marry* Alexa?' Rosanna's voice was scarcely audible.

'What!' Stuart positively bellowed. 'Marry *her* when I'm in love with *you*—do you think I'm mad?'

In one great stride he was behind her, his strong hands on her shoulders turning her to face him, the roses scattering all over the working surface around the sink.

'Awkward as I am,' he said, calming down a little, 'I love you very dearly. . .more, much more than I can say. You fill my heart, my thoughts, my very being.' Bending his head towards her, he kissed her lovingly, longingly.

Rosanna felt happiness flooding through her from head to toe.

'Now, what about this wedding?' Stuart asked softly after a few precious moments.

'Your grandfather's?'

'No, that's being taken care of. I mean yours. Would you want a double wedding?'

She shook her head. 'No, I'd want to marry in our hospital chapel,' she said dreamily. 'A white wedding, roses everywhere—Mr Hurst to give me away, Kevin as best man, hospital staff forming a guard of honour. . .'

'Holding crutches aloft?'

She laughed. 'Anything but scalpels and retractors!'

'But haven't you forgotten something—shouldn't there be a bridegroom?'

'Oh, dear, does there have to be? I haven't been proposed to yet!'

'Maybe Admin would advertise for one for you,' Stuart suggested. 'But if not,' he added with a beguiling pretence of humility, 'Would I do?'

PENNY JORDAN

A
COLLECTION

From the bestselling author of *Power Play*, *Silver* and *The Hidden Years* comes a special collection of three early novels, beautifully presented in one volume.

Featuring:

SHADOW MARRIAGE
MAN-HATER
PASSIONATE PROTECTION

Available from May 1992   Priced £4.99

W●RLDWIDE

— MEDICAL ROMANCE —

The books for enjoyment this month are:

THE SINGAPORE AFFAIR Kathleen Farrell
CAROLINE'S CONQUEST Hazel Fisher
A PLACE OF REFUGE Margaret Holt
THAT SPECIAL JOY Betty Beaty

♥ ♥ ♥ ♥ ♥

Treats in store!

Watch next month for the following absorbing stories:

MORE THAN TIME Caroline Anderson
LOVING QUEST Frances Crowne
CLOSER TO A STRANGER Lilian Darcy
DIAMONDS FROM DR DALY Angela Devine